HEARTS *of* AMISH COUNTRY™

Annie's SEARCH

Jerry Eicher

Annie's®

AnniesFiction.com

Library of Congress-in-Publication Data
Annie's Search/ by Jerry Eicher
p. cm.
I. Title
2017954743

AnniesFiction.com
(800) 282-6643
Hearts of Amish Country™
Series Creator: Shari Lohner
Series Editor: Janice Tate

10 11 12 13 14 | Printed in China | 9 8 7 6 5 4 3 2 1

1

An hour after dawn Annie Miller pushed open the front door of the small store set back from the narrow gravel road that ran past the Amish farmstead. The homemade timbered frame squealed on its hinges and came to rest against the back wall with a thump. The screen door slapped shut behind Annie. A leather strap dangled near the knob, but the fastener was only needed on days when the wind blasted across the rolling hills of southern Nebraska. The morning promised soft breezes and warm spring air from the south. There was not a thundercloud in the sky.

Annie paused to tuck a loose strand of hair back under her *Kapp*. Lily would be gardening today. Under her sister's tender care the plot of land beside the house would produce abundantly.

A smile played on Annie's face. How peaceful life was in the small Amish community nestled among the hollows and dirt roads outside Pawnee City. The town of Table Rock lay to the north within easy driving distance for a buggy. Here, the English and the Amish worlds lay side by side without conflict. The community only had two districts, but what it lacked in size, it made up for with dedication to the cause. Life was not always easy in Nebraska, with the cold winters and the meager soil. These were hardy farmers who had sought an escape from the rush of life in the larger Amish communities closer to the East Coast. Lancaster County, Pennsylvania could be reached in two or three days by bus, or in a long day or two with an English driver. Few made the trip except for funerals or a close relative's wedding.

Annie turned away from the screen door. This was the only life she had ever known. Not that she objected. The Millers were everything one could desire in a family: supportive, loving, and kind to one another. Her heart was the problem. There, reason, logic, and acceptance didn't make much of an impact.

She had surrendered her situation to the Lord's will a long time ago, and she was thankful for *Mamm* and *Daett*, who had adopted her as an infant and had raised her in the community.

Annie looked up as an English automobile pulled in the driveway. They must have noticed the small sign in the yard, *Annie's Amish Store*. Daett had dug the postholes for her, and Edwin, the oldest brother after her younger sister, Lily, had nailed the boards together. She had applied the paint. They had worked together, as always.

Annie stepped outside and waved to the elderly couple climbing out of their car.

"Is this Annie's Amish Store?" the woman called.

"It is, and *goot* morning."

"Good morning!" The woman approached with her husband in tow. "I'm Carlene, and you must be Annie."

"I am," Annie laughed. "You are out bright and early."

Carlene glowed. "Bill and I are feeling young this morning. It is spring and we are seeing a bit of Amish Country in the most unexpected of places, our own Nebraska!"

"So you live in the area?" Annie held the screen door wide.

"Yes." Carlene's smile filled her face. "We moved here after Bill retired from the military." Bill nodded a greeting. "He gives guided tours over at the Strategic Air Command & Aerospace Museum. I found your community on the Internet."

"Aerospace Museum?" Annie said, leading the way inside. "That sounds interesting."

The couple seemed not to hear, moving slowly down the aisles of bulk food and handmade Amish crafts.

"Do you have Amish baked goods?" Carlene asked.

"I'm afraid not." Annie made a face. "But I do have the ingredients."

"And recipes maybe?"

"Yes, I sell cookbooks." Annie motioned to the back of the store.

"I have always wanted to make Amish pastries." Carlene's face filled with rapture.

Bill chuckled. "You should stick with buying from people who know what they are doing."

Carlene slapped him playfully on the arm. "Bill has great confidence in my cooking—if it comes from a can."

They laughed together and Annie joined in.

"Everyone has their strong points," Annie allowed. "Obviously I'm Amish, and was taught how to cook, but I know nothing about what happens at the Strategic Air Command & Aerospace Museum."

Bill grinned. "You should come up someday, and bring your friends. I would like having Amish on my tour. I give them on the hour most days. You could call ahead and make sure I'm there that day."

Annie hesitated. "We'll have to see, but thanks for the offer."

Bill noticed her reluctance. "There isn't an Amish rule against such things, is there?"

"Not really, I guess. We are simply encouraged to stay close to home. Marriage and family are high priorities."

Bill smiled. "I meant no offense. I have the highest respect for the Amish culture."

"A military life doesn't exclude us seeing the value in other ways of doing things," Carlene chimed in.

"It's okay," Annie told them. "You didn't offend me."

"Good. We're not here to tempt you." Carlene's brilliant smile was back. "Now back to that recipe. I'll buy the cookbook, but could I beg a pie recipe off of you—maybe cherry? I'll gladly pay extra."

"There's no need for that," Annie assured her. "I'll run and get the recipe from the house. I have a notepad under the counter, and we can make a copy."

The friendly couple smiled as Annie rushed out of the store. Everything she had told them was true. The community did value home and family. At her age she should be married, or at least engaged. Many had been interested in the Millers' elder daughter, but she had declined their offers. Henry Hochstetler was the latest, and he hadn't given up yet. How did one explain such things? Tell them that she was adopted, that her heart wished to find her birth Mamm before she settled down as someone's *Frau*?

Annie burst into the kitchen.

Mamm looked up from her work at the kitchen sink. "Is everything okay, Annie?"

"The couple in the car. They want a recipe. The cherry pie recipe." The words came out in short spurts as Annie tried to catch her breath.

Mamm nodded. "You know where it is."

Annie pulled open the familiar drawer and grabbed the faded cookbook. "Thanks."

She dashed out of the house, clutching the pages to her chest, passing Lily, who was pushing a wheelbarrow filled with gardening implements toward the garden. Lily looked puzzled, which in no way surprised Annie. Annie knew that she was a mystery to her family. There were other adopted English children in the community, who married and settled down without a backward glance. Why was she different?

"I'm back!" Annie exclaimed, and the screen door slammed behind her.

Carlene had her purchases lined up on the counter: flour, brown sugar, seasoning, and the cookbook from the store. "This is so nice of you, Annie."

"It's not a problem." Annie began to write, copying the recipe on the tablet.

Carlene watched over Annie's shoulder for a moment to check the ingredients before she scurried back to the shelves for further purchases.

Lily dropped the handles of the wheelbarrow near the freshly worked ground. The thick layer of chicken manure she had scattered over the plowed ground had disappeared. She took a hoe and scratched the surface of the soil. The edge of the metal sank in with little effort.

"Goot job, Edwin." Lily smiled. "But what did I expect from my brother?"

The vehicle behind her by Annie's little store roared to life, and Lily turned to watch the elderly couple drive away. She sighed. Much as she loved her older sister, Annie brought a feeling of uncertainty to the otherwise stable Miller family. Annie didn't intend to. She had a goot heart and tried hard to fit into the community's life, but there was always something not quite right.

Everyone in the community knew that Annie had been adopted, and everyone was at peace about it. Except Annie. Annie had wanted to find her English birth Mamm since she could remember. No attempts at persuasion had changed her mind. Annie would be twenty-one soon, when her parents had promised she could embark on her long-awaited search. Perhaps peace would come if she could find her birth Mamm. There were, of course, plenty of dangers associated with that plan, which was why Mamm and Daett objected, along with everyone else in the community. Wandering the earth in search of healing for your heart was not what the Amish did. Peace, contentment, and acceptance were cardinal virtues and highly prized.

On that count, Lily passed the test. Everyone knew she was perfectly happy with the life the Lord had given her. With such a record she should be wed by now, and have a garden of her own this spring. Perhaps even a young one arriving this summer.

Lily whacked the hoe into the ground. She didn't want to wed any man except Jesse Yoder, and he had taken it upon himself to spend his *Rumspringa*—the time that most Amish youth experienced the English world—in the Amish communities of northern Indiana for the past three years. No one had heard from Jesse in an awfully long time. Could it be the man planned never to return? Even if he did, she had no claim on him. Other than a few smiles, Jesse had never responded to her overtures. Maybe he didn't care for gardens, the stability of the community, and *Kinner*—the children that were at the heart of Amish life. What else explained his long absence?

Lily dug her hoe deep into the ground. *This infatuation with Jesse must end*. If Jesse would return and wed some other girl, maybe Lily could let go. Or if they received word that Jesse had married an English woman. In the meantime, what was she supposed to do? She had been so certain once, back when they attended the little one-room schoolhouse and Jesse finally returned her smiles. But Jesse's heart could not have pounded like hers. Otherwise he would not have left the community. Neither had Jesse waited in breathless hope for a kind word from her lips. But then again, why would he?

Lily stared dreamily at the distant horizon. She had been named after Mamm because of Mamm's great joy that she had borne a child after many years of barrenness. *Lily* was short for *Lilliana* to avoid confusion. She was plain, common, ordinary Lily, the natural-born daughter of Enos and Lilliana Miller. That she should fall in love with Jesse Yoder, the most dashing, handsome, and wild Amish man in the community, made no sense. But she had. Didn't opposites attract? Maybe she was exactly what Jesse needed—if only Jesse could be persuaded.

Lily swung the hoe again, and the wooden handle protested with a soft crack. She ran her hand down the length. No splinters stuck into her fingers, so she had not broken anything. Damaging a hoe in her frustrations would be disastrous, but so was her inability to forget Jesse Yoder. Why couldn't she? The man had shown his feelings when he left the community for his Rumspringa. Jesse intended to keep himself and whatever he was doing out of the community's sight. Northern Indiana had one of the largest Amish communities in North America, and hundreds of youth took their Rumspringa there. It was a goot place to hide. That was easy to figure out. But she would forgive Jesse for whatever had happened in Indiana once he had returned to the community. Annie wasn't her sister by birth, but on this point they were bound together. She couldn't forget Jesse, and Annie couldn't forget her birth Mamm. Only the Lord could untangle those knots of the heart, and so far the Almighty had been silent on both subjects.

Perhaps she should pray more? She had often in the past, but nothing changed. In the meantime, Robert Schlabach gave her the cutest smiles at the hymn singings on Sunday evenings. He tried his best to win her affections whenever he had the chance, and the man would not wait forever. She might have to accept the inevitable soon, and Robert wasn't a bad catch. Perhaps she should comfort herself with that thought and return Robert's smiles. That would make Mamm and Daett happy. Lily knew they prayed daily for contentment in both of their daughters' lives.

"We must all accept the Lord's will in our lives," Mamm had told them often. "When we do, the heart always follows."

Lily sighed and pounded a stake in the ground with her shovel. She tied the string and moved across the garden, running the line behind her. Robert Schlabach was exactly the kind of man she *should* fall in love with—a farmer like his Daett and his grandfather before him, steady, humble, and handsome in an earthy sort of way. Robert would make a great Daett for any little ones the Lord gave them. Maybe if she could cross paths with Jesse again and see how much time had changed both of them, her heart would come to its senses.

Lily beat in the stake at the other end of the garden and fastened the string. The long line stretched across the dark ground. The earth was at peace, crumbled into submission by Edwin's harrow. She should be like that: accepting the Lord's will, returning Robert's affections, welcoming him into her life. Robert wouldn't mind that her heart still wondered about Jesse. She was the one who minded. She was the one who couldn't find peace.

That evening, Jesse Yoder entered the small third-floor apartment in the town of Goshen, Indiana. He threw his lunch box on the living room floor and settled on the couch with a groan. Rumspringa had its thrills, but after three years of wild weekend parties, home in Nebraska had begun to sound attractive. He had once planned to leave the community, where nothing ever happened, behind him for goot. Yolanda Wright, a girl he had met in northern Indiana, had cemented his determination. Now Yolanda was gone, and his heart was ripped from his chest.

The accident hadn't been entirely his fault. There had been the dog, their speed, and the curve in the road. He should have been more careful, but their joy in each other had distracted him. In an instant, Yolanda was dead, and he was left to grieve alone, far from the only home he knew, his family, his community.

Jesse was tired. He'd had enough of factory work and the long hours needed to finance his weekend life. If Rumspringa was intended as the time to discover what lay outside the boundaries of the Amish community, he had made the discovery—heartache, disappointment, and the excruciating pain of regret. The peace and quiet of southern Nebraska was bliss in comparison with life here. Maybe the time had arrived to call this quits and head back to the edge of the prairie.

But what then? Bachelors were frowned upon in the community. There, men took duties upon their shoulders, married wives, and raised families. That would be expected of him. Jesse stared at the ceiling. He should be able to find a Frau in the community. That was not the problem. After what he had experienced in northern Indiana, a steady, down-home Amish girl looked like the right choice. Life in the community could be drudgery if the heart was not fully there. That had been his problem, but maybe if he returned, his heart would follow.

On the other hand, he could ask his Amish cousins, the ones who had drawn him to northern Indiana in the first place, for a place to board. That would give him a taste of home, but the move would be temporary. His cousins had their own lives to live.

Jesse leaned back on the couch and a smile crept across his face. Back in Nebraska, Lily Miller had adored him in their school years. If ever there was a woman who was Amish to the depth of her soul, Lily fit the bill. Her adopted older sister, Annie, was another matter. Annie had plans that didn't involve family, community, and settling down. Maybe the girl had given them up and married, but he was doubtful. Lily was a different matter. By now that woman would certainly have said the wedding vows and have a houseful of little ones.

Jesse grinned. The perfect mental image of Lily was with a little one in her arms and several toddlers hiding in her apron. Back in their school days, he should have given the girl more attention, but he had never shared Lily's infatuation. They had seemed headed in opposite directions, and distance was the best choice. Now it was too late.

Jesse stood. There would be other available Amish women in the community, once he returned and made his intentions to settle down clear. One didn't have to fall in love to marry—that was the Amish way. He had been in love with Yolanda, and look where that had led. Better the community's standards where practicality was respected. He could make that choice. He could marry and settle down. Surely he would learn to love.

Jesse headed for the kitchen. He needed a distraction from dark thoughts, and he was hungry. Sandwiches were the extent of his cooking skills. After three years, he hated sandwiches. He should have stopped in at a fast food joint on the way home, but he hated fast food even more.

Amish cooking—now that he could live with. Mashed potatoes, gravy, a meat dish, boiled corn, perhaps green beans, and a tossed salad. Fresh bread—still steaming from the heat of the oven, the crust lathered with homemade butter, cut thick and spread with homemade strawberry jam.

"It's time to go home," Jesse muttered, opening the refrigerator door, "and find me an Amish wife."

2

The following week, Annie carried the covered casserole dish up the sidewalk to Deacon Bontrager's front door. Lily followed with two lemon cream pies in her hands. As the girls approached the small group of young people on the porch, a few of them glanced their way.

"He's looking at you," Lily teased, whispering over Annie's shoulder.

"And he's coming," Annie deadpanned, as Henry Hochstetler detached himself from the others and came down the steps.

"You should give him your warmest attentions," Lily advised.

Annie didn't reply. Henry was within earshot. Her red face already betrayed her, even if she had no intentions of following Lily's instructions.

"Goot evening," Henry greeted them. "You are both lovely tonight."

"And you are quite handsome and charming." Lily gave Henry her sweetest smile. "But the real news is Annie's lemon cream pies. Have you tasted them lately? They keep getting better and better and are so . . . oh!" Lily ended with a flourish that nearly sent the pies flying.

"Lily!" Annie chided.

Henry leaped forward, his arms extended to catch the delicacies. "That was close! Do you always toss goot pies around with such abandon?"

They laughed along with the young people back on the porch.

"You should taste Lily's meat casserole. That's what I have here," Annie told him. "Now that's cooking."

"I suppose I'll get to sample both of the Miller sisters' excellent cooking tonight," Henry allowed. "In the meantime could I have a word with you, Annie? Somewhere private?" He nodded toward the barn.

Annie hesitated. Clearly Henry wanted to speak about a possible date, and maybe even a marriage proposal. Since she usually avoided him, Henry might go for a home run if he succeeded in getting her alone with him.

"Annie will be thrilled to speak with you," Lily piped up. "Let me take these pies into the house and I'll be right back for the casserole."

Lily dashed off before Annie could protest, but what was the use? She might as well speak with Henry. He would insist until she accepted.

"How are things going on the farm this week?" she asked as they waited in discomfort.

Henry appeared at a loss for words. His mind was obviously on what he wanted to say once they were alone.

"Spring is here," he finally said. "And we're doing okay. The weather could be nicer I guess, but we shouldn't complain. With the cold weather hanging around, we might be spared a hot prairie summer."

"We might." She nodded. "I take it you don't like hot summers?"

He glanced at the house, but Lily still hadn't reappeared. "I do at times long for the cooler temperature of the East, but Nebraska has much going for it. I'm glad we live here."

"Winters are cold here and the summers are hot." Annie forced a smile. *Where is Lily?*

Henry's smile was tense. "We about went stir-crazy this past winter. Sitting around the stove waiting for the snow to melt gets old."

"Don't you like to read?"

He shrugged. "I guess there are books interesting enough to look into, but I haven't seen many of them."

"I see." Annie shifted the casserole.

"I'm back," Lily sang out, and Annie jumped. "Be nice," Lily whispered in Annie's ear as she took the casserole.

Annie turned to face Henry. "I guess I'm ready." She wasn't, but this might as well be faced cheerfully.

Henry led the way across the lawn with his hands in his pockets. Several men coming out of the barn passed them, big grins on their faces. Her face would soon blaze bright red if they didn't get out of sight. Judging by the heat she felt rising up her neck, it was already quite pink.

Henry chose the small lean-to beside the barn for the conversation. Several bales of hay were stacked high near the entrance, ready to feed the farm animals. Henry pulled out a bale for Annie to sit on before he settled on one himself.

Annie waited, her gaze fixed on the strings holding the hay bales together. This was Amish life. This was what she should want. And she did, but not yet. That was her internal conflict, which Henry could not know. Without that knowledge Henry wouldn't be persuaded by her arguments. If Henry would only wait until her heart was settled—until she had found her English Mamm—maybe she would take another look at him. But wait until when? She didn't know, and Amish men didn't tolerate hesitation at this stage in their lives. Henry would move on if she dallied.

Henry cleared his throat. "I don't know quite where to begin, Annie. From what I hear a lot of other men have asked you home on dates, and you declined. I don't understand that. You're almost twenty-one, and I won't pride myself thinking I'm the one you have been waiting for—at least I haven't gotten that impression."

"I—oh, Henry." Annie met his gaze. "I'm sure you are a decent man, and a great opportunity for some girl. I am honored that you would consider asking me for a date."

"But the answer would still be no?" His face was pained.

"What am I supposed to say, Henry? I really can't explain. But what if I asked for more time? A year maybe?"

He sighed. "Apparently you find me lacking in some area. What else could explain your rejection? I know that I'm not the most handsome man in the community, but I do know how to farm, and I'm a year older than you are. It's time I settled down. Aren't you ready yourself?"

"I have . . . I still . . ." She stopped. Explanations wouldn't work.

"Is there someone else?" he asked.

"No. Truly."

Obviously he didn't believe her from the skeptical look on his face. "I like you, Annie. I think we would be goot together. But if you disagree, I will demonstrate my lack of malice by informing this other man of your interest. It's a shame that you don't have a boyfriend."

"I'm okay," Annie assured him. "We don't want to go there."

"So there is someone? You are ashamed to say who it is?"

"There is not!" Annie forced a laugh. Maybe the truth would work. "I would like to find my English birth mother, Henry. That's been a dream of my heart for a long time, and I can't let go of it."

"You would jump the fence and join the English?" Horror filled Henry's face.

"No! See, that's what I mean. I want to remain Amish, but I want—no, I *need* to find her."

Sadness had replaced his horror. "Well, I guess I can understand that. Your heart may be in the right place, wanting to find your real Mamm. But you should know this will be a dangerous journey, Annie. You would be wise to stop looking back. The Millers did the Lord's will by taking you in. You are one of us, even though you were born English. Why can't you forget what you have never seen? Let me take you home on a date, Annie. You could learn to love me." He took her hand and held it tight.

"Henry." She swallowed hard. "I can't make any promises. You're right—I don't know where the search will take me, but I must go. I'm sorry. I shouldn't have asked you to wait. I know that."

His grip on her hand loosened. "Much as I like you, I am getting older. But that aside, this search does not bode well for your future.

As with all Amish men, I want a stable woman who will care for my future Kinner, if the Lord should so bless. We do not want women who trot the world looking for things they lack."

"I know." Annie stood. "We should get back to the house."

"I wish you would reconsider my offer. Perhaps in a week or so? I can wait that long. I won't tell anyone what you told me."

She shook her head. "Mamm and Daett already know. It's no secret. I hope you find the Frau you are looking for. In the meantime, would you like to attend my birthday party on Friday evening?"

Henry grunted an affirmative, and Annie followed him out of the lean-to, where she pasted on a brave smile for the walk back to the house.

Inside the house, Lily carried a plate of fresh bread from the kitchen toward the long dining room table.

"How are you tonight?" Robert Schlabach sidled up to her. "Let me carry those for you."

"I am perfectly capable," Lily protested. "I toss around hay bales in the summer and drive the six-horse team plowing."

Robert grinned. "You are something, but I already knew that. Will you let me help anyway?"

She gave in and handed the plate to him. "Don't spill the bread on the floor."

"Now who thinks someone can't handle a chore?"

Several girls near them giggled.

"You are making a scene," Lily scolded.

Robert's smile didn't fade. "I'll be expecting a fresh task after I finish with this plate."

Lily made a face behind his back and returned to the kitchen.

Here she had encouraged Annie not thirty minutes ago to accept Henry's attentions, and now she rejected her own opportunity at marriage and family. Maybe she should lead by example instead of lectures? All it would take was a few heartfelt smiles in Robert's direction and she would have a date after the hymn singing tonight.

"That Robert is getting really serious about you," one of the girls whispered in her ear.

Lily held her nose in the air and gathered up the bowl of heated green beans from the counter. Robert met her outside the kitchen doorway with his hands outstretched. She gave him the bowl, and he leaned closer. "You've worked hard enough tonight," he whispered. "I'll drop this off and then come sit with you."

Lily gave in with a quick nod. Why not? She could catch her breath if nothing else.

"There are empty chairs in the back." He motioned with his shaven chin. "I'll be with you in a second."

Several men gave Robert winks, but he didn't gloat over his conquest. The man had a sterling character as she already knew. Robert's reputation in the community was well established.

He returned and pulled out the chair for her before he seated himself. They sat shoulder to shoulder, inches apart in the crowded room.

"How's the spring farmwork going?" she asked.

He chuckled. "Goot for the most part. Of course, you can have problems anywhere. Two horses got into the feed bin last week. Thankfully there was only a partial bag of oats they could get into, and the damage was minimal. We had to walk them in the barnyard most of the morning before their bowels started to work again."

"Someone must have left open the gate, I suppose."

Robert sobered. "I know. I of all people should know better."

Lily pulled in her breath. "Sorry. I didn't mean it the way it sounded." She changed the subject. "How's your grandmother doing?"

Relief flickered on his face. "Okay, I think. The winter cold was hard on her, but she is moving about again. She is over ninety, you know."

"Spring does everyone goot." Lily gave him a bright smile. "I got our garden in last week."

"All by yourself?" Robert was clearly impressed.

"I had all day." Lily shrugged. "Mamm would rather take care of the house than work in the garden."

"But still—" Robert fell silent, his gaze fixed on the front door.

Lily turned for a better view and gasped. "Jesse Yoder!"

Robert stared at her. "Did you know he was back?"

"No. I . . . we . . ." Lily gave up and focused on breathing.

Robert would have to think what he wished. She couldn't hide her feelings. Not with a shock like this.

Jesse stepped behind the front door and out of sight for a moment. He had been gone for three years. What was he supposed to do? Wave his arms around and shout, "I'm home. Don't look at me"?

Two men approached and held out their hands in greeting.

"So you're back." The words were more statement than question.

Jesse shook their hands. "I guess so."

"For goot?"

"I think so." Jesse forced a smile.

His automobile was parked beside his Daett's barn until he could sell it. A concession made by his family in their delight that he—the prodigal son—had returned. He would be given time to sort things out.

In the meantime, he had walked up to Deacon Bontrager's place for the Sunday evening supper and hymn singing. He would be walking around the community until he could make a purchase of a horse and buggy.

"I'm glad you're home." Another man approached him. They shook hands.

He caught a glimpse of Lily's face as she sat beside Robert Schlabach. The woman was pale, as if she had seen a ghost. Maybe he was a ghost? Or a spirit from the past? Lily still appeared much the same—plain and rosy-cheeked, with a solid kind of beauty. That he had expected. If Lily wasn't married, she was obviously dating Robert Schlabach. He should go over and shake her hand, offer his congratulations, and move past any awkward moments from their past. But that would draw attention he didn't want. Better to leave Lily alone and focus on his hunger for Amish food, his desire for home, and his wish for the peace that exuded from a gathering like this.

Jesse worked his way up to the dining room table. The spread of food in front of him seemed to extend into the distance, a delight that overwhelmed his senses.

"I can see you are glad to be home." Someone pounded him on the back.

Jesse joined in the laughter. "You can say that again."

Would this moment have been any better if he had arrived while Lily was still available? He glanced over his shoulder. Lily had her head down and was talking with Robert. She appeared to have recovered her color.

Maybe this moment couldn't be improved, even the slightest bit.

3

The birthday party invitations had been given in whispered conversations after the Sunday evening hymn singing.

Friday afternoon had arrived, and Annie left the oven door open while she transferred the cherry pie to the counter with a hot pad. Light-brown crust rimmed the pan, with gooey red goodness rising from the center through the star-shaped holes in the dough. Annie set the pie down and turned on her heel to transport the second one from the oven. Lily would come in any moment through the washroom that connected the kitchen to the outdoors.

Tonight would be a joyous occasion but tempered by sadness. She would try not to think of the future on this happy evening. What might lie out there in the unknown world of the English would come later. The less said about her planned venture, the better. She knew Mamm and Daett hoped the gathering to celebrate her official coming of age would remind her of the blessings the community offered and banish any unrest that stirred in her soul. She had not tried to dissuade them of their hopes. It was a touchy subject. She was a Miller, but she was adopted. Nothing could change that.

The washroom door burst open and Lily entered the kitchen, wiping her wet hands on her apron.

"Are you done in the garden?" Annie asked.

Lily's face glowed with happiness. "Oh Annie, it's so goot to work outside on a warm spring day. The weeds are just popping, and so is everything else. The garden will produce the Lord's bounty again this year. I'm sure of it."

Annie set the last pie on the table. "Your loving care can make anything blossom."

"You are much better than I am at cooking." Lily returned the compliment at once. "Will I spoil your birthday party if I help in the kitchen?"

Annie laughed. "Don't be silly. I'm behind and your help would be greatly appreciated. I don't want the first arrivals to catch me with my hands still in the dough. What a sight that would be."

Lily smiled but soon sobered. "Don't you think that was a mistake on Sunday evening at Deacon Bontrager's, Annie? I haven't had a chance to mention something, but Henry looked so disappointed after he came into the house."

"I . . ." Annie made a face. "I couldn't accept a date with Henry, Lily. My heart just isn't there yet. Once Henry knew my plans, he changed his tune. That's just how Amish men are. So that's that." Annie glanced back at the counter. "Let's see. The chocolate cakes and lemon bars. That should be about it."

Lily sighed and pulled on a clean apron. "You know that your chances of finding your birth Mamm aren't very goot. Mamm and Daett don't know anything about her or where you came from, at least that they've told us. And even if they know something, it probably won't be enough for you to actually find her."

Annie nodded. That was the problem—the many unknowns. Amish life didn't tolerate unknowns. Not the kind created by willful choices. That was how her search for her real Mamm would appear to everyone—self-expression that courted disaster, to say nothing of what the end of the search might reveal. Would she abandon Amish life if her English Mamm welcomed her with open arms?

"What if you find your Mamm?" Lily echoed the unspoken fear. "You are my sister, but what if you forget that? What if you meet someone out there who loves you dearly and wants you to stay?"

"I could never forget you," Annie protested, "or Mamm and Daett, or my life here. Look at me. I'm Amish, right? That's what I'll always be." Annie stared at the recipe, as if the words on the page could answer.

Lily slipped her arm around Annie's shoulder and pulled her close. "I know that, and so do Mamm and Daett—sort of, at least. The others have doubts, and you can't blame them, Annie. They don't know you that well, and you have turned down offers of dates from so many." Lily ticked off the names on her fingers. "Lavon, James, Titus, and now Henry." Lily raised her eyebrows. "I've only had Robert Schlabach interested in me, someone who doesn't feel like I do." Lily bit her lower lip and hurried on. "Then Jesse walks in after three long years to see me sitting beside Robert, looking cozy and settled. Why didn't I refuse Robert's request to sit beside him when I had the chance? If Jesse only knew."

"Sometimes men figure these things out," Annie comforted Lily. "He did notice you, didn't he?"

Lily's face darkened. "*Yah*, Jesse immediately looked right at us. That's the problem. He actually remembered me, but I spoiled the moment when the door to Jesse's heart could have been open. I just know I did."

Annie moved the pies to the cupboard. "Did you have something going with Jesse before he left? Perhaps some unspoken agreement?"

Lily wrinkled her forehead. "Not really. The feelings were one-sided, I think. But I couldn't give up my hope those years that Jesse was gone." Lily attempted a smile. "And Jesse did remember me."

Annie measured out the flour into a large bowl before she answered. "Then we will pray the Lord's will be done."

"He was also looking at you," Lily said quietly.

Annie's head came up with a start. "Who was?"

"Jesse! He couldn't take his eyes off of you after supper."

Annie laughed. "Don't start with that, Lily. I have other things on my mind."

"So you did notice?"

"I was busy helping with the cooking. Jesse was probably looking at all the available girls now that he's back from Rumspringa."

Lily was clearly not convinced. "Anyway," she said, "I hope you don't object that I invited Jesse to the party tonight. I couldn't resist."

"You spoke with him?" Annie stared. "When did you have the chance?"

"After the hymn singing, there were others talking to him. I caught a quiet moment, and he accepted." Lily attempted a smile. "Though probably not because of me."

"You underrate yourself completely. You are exactly the wife Jesse needs. He's settling down in the community, and you can raise a garden like no one I've ever seen. You can work the fields, the kitchen, everywhere. I'm glad you asked him to come."

"So you think I still have a chance?"

"Lily, please. Of course you do." Annie gave her sister a quick kiss on the cheek. "And don't worry about me. I have my plate completely full, even if Jesse did look at me."

Lily hugged herself. "Thank you for saying that, Annie. You are such a *wunderbah* sister."

Annie raised her flour-covered spoon. "To the blossoming of Jesse and Lily's love."

Lily giggled and rushed about the kitchen.

Two hours later, the first of the buggies rolled into the Millers' driveway. Lily stood beside the barn with Annie, ready to greet the arrivals.

"Goot evening," Lily called out to the lead buggy.

Annie leaned over to whisper, "That's Henry's buggy. I hope he's not too upset."

"He came," Lily whispered back. "He would still take you on a date, I'm sure."

Annie didn't answer as they approached the buggies. Henry had climbed down with his sister Mary beside him.

"How are you tonight?" Lily asked Mary, who was still standing beside her brother's buggy.

"Okay," Mary answered. "Henry's a little grumpy, but he came."

They both glanced at Henry and Annie, who were busy unhitching Henry's horse. "I did my part to convince her." Lily let the sentence hang.

"Do you think there is hope then? My heart melts for Henry. He's fallen quite deeply for the girl."

"I don't think so." Lily made a face. "Annie hasn't given me any reason to believe that she might change her mind."

Mary pressed a wrinkle out of her white apron. "Does Annie really plan to set out on a search for her birth Mamm?"

"Yah. She's completely set on it."

Mary pulled her out of sight behind the buggy. "Can't Annie see what a chance she is being offered? Henry could have taken a Frau by now. There have been plenty of opportunities, but he has waited. Why, I didn't know, but clearly the man was getting up his courage to ask Annie home on a date. Now his plans are broken."

Lily glanced at Henry, who was leading his horse to the barn. "Annie is a sweet girl. I can understand why Henry would feel that way."

"You don't have your bonnet set for him, do you?"

"I do not!" Lily retorted as another buggy pulled in the driveway.

Mary appeared unconvinced. She turned on her heel and scurried up the sidewalk.

Lily moved to the next buggy and planted a smile on her face. "Goot evening. How is everyone tonight?"

Cousin Jerome and his two sisters climbed down. With a wave of their hands, Millie and Eunice headed up the walk. Lily took off the tug on her side of the buggy.

"Where are the men?" Jerome asked.

"Why? Don't you like a woman unhitching the horse for you?" Lily teased.

Jerome grinned. "You know I like you just fine, cousin. Just checking on why the Miller brothers are shirking their duties."

"Charles is still not back from town. They ran out of grease for the wagon wheels this afternoon, I think. And Edwin's in the barn directing the horse traffic."

Jerome led his horse forward while Lily held the shafts. "Must be an awful difficult knot to untangle."

"I know. Maybe Edwin's consoling Henry over his loss on Sunday evening."

"I heard." Jerome grimaced. "Another heart broken."

"Surely you're not on the list of Annie's admirers." Lily glared at him. "Tell me this isn't true. Annie is your cousin."

He snorted. "Annie also *isn't* my cousin. Remember that."

Lily stared after Jerome's retreating back. Did Jerome care for Annie? He had never given any indication. What made the men flock around her sister? She could understand in a way—but Jerome? Cousin or no cousin, that was too much. If Annie needed to find her birth Mamm, she had better do it sooner rather than later so she could heal and settle down in the community with a decent man. This had gone on long enough.

Maybe Lily could help. But how? She knew little about the English world that lay outside the boundaries of the community. Jesse, on the other hand, knew plenty. Maybe, just maybe, Jesse would be willing to do Annie a favor before he settled down for goot, and Lily could tag along on the trip. Healing might come to their hearts—a fresh start. Jesse wouldn't have much to lose, but she knew Annie wouldn't ask him. Lily would have to do it for her sister. And if she were honest, for herself.

Another buggy came in the driveway, and Lily hurried toward it. Robert Schlabach and his sister Rebecca had arrived. She should at least be friendly to the man.

"Goot evening," Lily called out.

Robert climbed down from his buggy before he answered. "Goot to see you, Lily."

"And you as well." She gave him a warm smile.

He nodded but said nothing more.

Thirty minutes later, Jesse Yoder drove his new horse and buggy to the Millers' place at a brisk clip. He had found a horse and wasn't walking tonight, but he would still be late for Annie's birthday party. He could use the excuse that he hadn't been around a horse and buggy for three years. There was some truth to that. While he was gone, he had thoroughly immersed himself in the English world, but one did not forget how to drive a horse and buggy in that amount of time. No, Jesse was late because he had dawdled, thinking about Lily's invitation. How would she interpret his acceptance? Would she think he was interested in her romantically? Lily would know he was in need of a Frau now that he had returned to the community. She would expect practicality from him. They were both older and ready to settle down. Lily was what he wanted—in theory. For a moment after he had walked into Deacon Bontrager's home on Sunday evening, he had thought her engaged to Robert Schlabach. Several of the men had soon enlightened him otherwise.

Did Lily know that her adopted sister had caught his eye? Likely not, or Lily wouldn't have whispered the birthday invitation to him later in the evening. He had told her he might come, but he had made no promises.

Jesse settled back into the buggy seat and jiggled the reins. Annie intrigued him. But why? Annie wasn't like Yolanda—or was she? He hadn't noticed Annie in that way before he left for Rumspringa. There had been Lily and several others who had gotten his attention. All but Lily were married now. Lily would help him forget Yolanda, but what about Annie?

Annie appeared the perfect vision of a demure Amish maiden, but in her heart Annie was still part English. The girl couldn't help that.

Jesse hung on to the reins as he turned his buggy into the Millers' driveway. Perhaps he wanted both the English life and the community life. But such a thing was impossible! Or was it?

Jesse pulled to a stop by the barn. A long line of buggies were parked along the fencerow, but no one was in sight. He would have to unhitch by himself. He was certain a food-laden table awaited him inside the house, with dishes that made a man's mouth water. He should be thankful and accept what Lily offered him.

Jesse sighed and stepped down from the buggy.

4

The following Saturday afternoon, during the weekly cleaning of the Millers' old farmhouse, Annie took one last swipe at the spiderwebs in the upstairs bedroom. Where had they come from? Probably through a break in the screen, now that warm spring weather had arrived and the window sash was propped open. Annie set her broom down and walked closer to inspect the screen. Every inch appeared in place.

Annie leaned on the windowpane with both hands. Below her the rolling Nebraska countryside stretched into the distance. A wagon and a team of horses bounced southward on the gravel road. Her brother Charles gripped the reins tightly, leaning back to hold the eager animals. This was her life, the one she had always known. Why couldn't she be content to leave the past alone?

She hadn't said anything since the birthday party, where Henry had again made his affections for her plain. The man had found a way to hang by her side the entire evening, but he hadn't been unpleasant, and the party had been a goot time. This happiness could continue with Henry as her husband. He was a steady man and would keep their family supplied with the staples of life. But would her heart be happy? Could she settle for life in the community without knowing and meeting the woman who was her real Mamm? There were things she wanted desperately to know. What did her Mamm look like? Why did she give up her child for adoption? Did she regret the decision to let Annie go?

Annie took a deep breath and ran her hand over the screen. The corner gave way under the pressure of her hand to reveal a long slit in the screen. So this was the problem. Spiders and other insects had not missed the weak point hidden from her eyes.

Annie jerked her hand back from the screen. Was she like that? Was there a flaw in her that would give way under pressure? Annie stifled a cry of alarm and hurried out of the bedroom and down the stairs.

"Annie, is that you?" Mamm called from the kitchen.

Annie paused to compose herself before she answered. "Yah."

"What are you doing?" Mamm peered around the corner.

Annie pasted on a smile. "Edwin's screen has a break, and the spiders are having a field day. I'm almost done with the upstairs cleaning."

Mamm pointed to the desk drawer. "I think there's duct tape in there."

"Any clear tape?"

Mamm shook her head, and Annie dug in the drawer.

"We'd like to talk with you, Daett and I," Mamm said. "He's coming in from the fields in a few minutes."

Annie's hand clutched the roll of tape. "On a Saturday afternoon?"

"I know we're busy getting ready for the Lord's Day, but the little ones are outside playing in the nice weather, and your brothers are in the fields. We don't want to rush the conversation or have listening ears."

Annie stood upright. "I am so sorry about all this. You have been nothing but kind to me, so I'm not blaming you."

"Just finish upstairs and come back down," Mamm said, hushing her.

"Can Lily be with us?"

"Lily?" Mamm appeared puzzled.

"Lily knows everything about my plans." The point was difficult to explain.

"I guess so, but Lily doesn't have to know if you don't want her to."

"I would like her input. If Lily could be here, that would be goot." Annie didn't wait for an answer, but fled upstairs with the tape held tight.

She almost tripped over the broom propped against the bedroom door and steadied herself against the window frame for a moment. Charles and his team were a speck in the distance, ready to disappear into the trees on the other side of a stream that flowed through their small valley. Annie got on her knees in front of the screen and ran out a piece of tape with trembling hands. She paused to lay the roll on the hardwood floor. After a deep breath, Annie pressed the piece of tape against the screen. The wire membrane gave way, and the tape slipped from the edges. How was this to work? Her vision blurred.

Annie sat on the floor as tears stung her eyes. It was not like her to become emotional over a torn screen. With a groan, Annie pushed herself up from the floor and headed across the hall to her bedroom. She grabbed the first needle in sight with thread dangling from its eye. The blue color was wrong, but what did it matter? Back in Edwin's bedroom, she lowered herself to her knees and placed her elbows on the windowsill to stitch the torn edges together.

Annie leaned back, surveying her work. Not perfect, but the spiders would stay outdoors where they belonged. *This is what I need. Stitches on my heart.* The tears burned again. Mamm and Daett had not caused her wound, but they also lacked the power to mend it. Others were responsible for the injury, so others must hold the needle and thread that could pull the pieces of her heart together. That was why she had to find her English Mamm.

But what direction did one go on this journey? She only knew she had to begin somewhere—anywhere—on a search that might take years.

Annie took the stairs slowly, pausing to wipe her eyes. There would be enough tears shed this afternoon. She shouldn't be ashamed though. Love of family was a lynchpin of the community's existence.

Likely that was the reason her planned search for her birth Mamm was tolerated. Otherwise Deacon Bontrager would have made a trip over to the Millers' house in his buggy a long time ago to express the ministry's displeasure over her plans. She would be given room but not too much. The way would be narrow, and she would traverse it at her own risk. If mistakes were made, there would be no Henry Hochstetler waiting with open arms upon her return. Henry might already have decided he would move on. She would likely return to find him enraptured with the attentions of some other girl from the community.

Annie pushed open the stairwell door and stepped into the living room. Daett sat on his rocker, with Mamm beside him. Their eyes were filled with sadness.

"I'll call Lily." Mamm stood. "She's in the garden."

Annie avoided Daett's gaze. She seated herself on the old couch, not entirely sure she was ready for the emotions that soon would follow.

Outside in the bright sunshine, Lily pulled the weeds carefully from around the tender carrot plants. She tossed the offending guests aside and patted the disturbed earth back into place. In a few weeks the first of the lettuce could be picked. The earth's offering of green beans and tomatoes would not be far behind. What joy stirred in her heart at the bounty the Lord gave each year. Not so long ago, in the midst of the winter's snow, the smell of summer on the afternoon breezes had been a distant memory.

"Lily," Mamm called from the front porch.

Lily jerked her head up. "Yah?"

"Can you come in?"

"I'll put the hoe away," Lily called back, already headed for the barn.

Lily entered through the creaking door, and Edwin peered at her from around the feed bin. "Why does Mamm want you in the house?"

"I don't know."

"Something serious then?"

"You heard how she sounded."

"Is Annie up to something?"

"Probably," Lily hazarded a guess. "We all knew this was coming after Annie's twenty-first birthday."

"I wish she would settle down. She's soiling our reputation in the community."

Lily nodded. Edwin loved his adopted sister, but everyone's nerves were on edge.

"Maybe this will soon be over," she suggested.

Edwin shrugged and disappeared around the corner of the grain bin. Lily hung the hoe on its nail on the barn wall and hurried back outside. Daett and Mamm sat with sober faces on their rockers when she entered the house, with Annie sitting downcast beside them on the couch. Lily had guessed correctly.

Daett cleared his throat once Lily was seated. Annie appeared close to tears, and Lily's heart stirred. What would she do if she were in Annie's shoes? Lily gave her sister a quick squeeze on the arm.

"Annie wanted you in on this conversation," Daett began. "And I guess that answers my first question. You still intend to set out on a search for your birth Mamm, Annie?"

A quick nod came from Annie, and tears splattered her apron.

"How exactly do you plan to accomplish this search?" Daett continued. "None of us knows who your birth Mamm is or where she lives."

"I know," Annie squeaked.

"Not only is there the question of how, there is the question of where, and how long? There are so many questions, daughter, I cannot begin to name them. So much can happen out there, and so many things can go wrong. And what if you do find her? What will that accomplish?"

"Careful, Enos," Mamm warned. "The girl's heart is tender."

"I'm sorry," Daett demurred. "I did not mean to sound unkind, but the point is still that you have much more to lose than you have to gain. At least that's how it seems to me."

Annie's voice caught. "I've tried to tell myself the same thing, and I am grateful for all you and Mamm have given me, but there's a hole in my heart that needs mending." Annie gulped. "I'm sorry. You don't know how sorry I am."

"You are not to blame, dear," Mamm comforted her. "Others made choices that affected you, and deeply, but I, too, question the wisdom of this search. Can you not accept everything the Lord has given you and be satisfied? Look at how Henry Hochstetler adores you." Mamm's face brightened. "You have turned down a lot of men. I don't say that I blamed you on most of them, but Henry is quite a catch, Annie. You could do no better."

"I'm not trying to do better," Annie managed. "I'm trying to do what's right, but my heart will not settle down until I know for sure if my real Mamm is alive, and if she cares about me." Annie's voice ended in a whimper.

"I don't blame you for wanting to find her," Mamm said. "But where will you begin? That's the first question. You have to be practical."

"Then you must help her begin." Lily jumped into the conversation. "You promised you would tell Annie everything you knew. Where did you find Annie? A children's home? An adoption agency? She wasn't dropped on your doorstep one morning."

There was silence from Mamm and Daett. Annie leaned forward on the couch, her face eager. "You do know, don't you?"

Mamm glanced at Daett, who finally spoke. "We did promise to tell you what we know—which isn't much—but I'm struggling now. How is this to help?"

"Just tell her," Lily said. "Let Annie decide."

"Should we?" Daett glanced at Mamm.

"You should, Enos," Mamm replied. "We owe her that much, and we did promise."

Daett stroked his beard for a long time before he answered. "The midwife in Lancaster County, Olivia Raber—she's very old now—brought you to us and asked whether we would take you in. 'The fewer questions asked, the better for everyone,' she said. That was the agreement, and we have seen no reason to think otherwise since."

"Then Annie could visit Olivia Raber and begin there," Lily suggested.

"She's in Lancaster County, which is quite a distance from here," Daett replied.

"I want to go—I *must* go." Annie clasped her hands tightly on her lap. "This is the first ray of light to shine on my heart in a long time."

Daett ignored Annie to fix his gaze on Lily. "Why are you in this?"

Lily shrugged. "I don't know. I care about Annie, and she needs help. Her heart is like a tender plant in my garden, but the weeds are choking her. We need to help Annie pull the weeds."

There was a sob from Annie as Mamm regarded Lily with a steady gaze. Daett grunted but said nothing.

"I think we should ask Jesse Yoder to help us," Lily blurted. "Jesse could take us to Lancaster County before he gets rid of his automobile. I saw it parked in front of the Yoders' barn. I think Jesse would do it if we asked him."

Silence gripped the room as everyone stared at her.

"We should," Lily insisted.

Mamm and Daett turned to Annie, who shrugged. "I'll take any help I can get."

Jesse stood by the barn door, listening to the distant beat of horse hooves on the gravel road. These were the sounds of home after the years he had spent in cramped apartments with the roar of English city life outside his window. He drew a long breath and listened again. The *clip-clops* were the peaceful rhythm of Amish life he had come to embrace again. The sound grew louder, and he glimpsed the top of the approaching buggy. He waited, ready to wave, but the horse slowed and turned into the driveway.

Visitors? Perhaps Deacon Bontrager?

This was a Saturday afternoon, when the deacon sallied forth on church work, rebuking erring members and keeping the sheep in line—an unpleasant but necessary part of community life. He had almost forgotten. Well, the music must be faced. Someone must have complained about his car.

Jesse pasted on a smile and stepped forward. The buggy stopped and a skirt came down the step instead of pant legs. So much for his presumptuousness. He should have taken a better look through the plastic windshield before he drew conclusions.

"Goot afternoon," he called.

Another dress appeared, and Annie Miller joined Lily beside the buggy. Their horse stood with its head lowered, waiting. Both sisters wore smiles, but their smiles didn't reach their eyes.

"I thought you were the deacon," he teased, and warmth returned to their faces.

"We were thinking you need to make a church confession tomorrow," Lily replied.

"I am sure I have plenty to confess," he allowed, and joined in their laughter.

Lily glanced at Annie. "The truth is we're not here for that."

"Okay." He tilted his head.

"Would you take us to Pennsylvania on a search for Annie's birth Mamm?" Lily blurted out.

"Lily," Annie chided. "You didn't have to come right out and say it."

Jesse chuckled. "No offense taken."

"So you will do it?" Lily's gaze was intense.

"I didn't say that," he said.

"I—I'm so sorry," Annie sputtered. "This was not wise, I know. I shouldn't have agreed to come. You have plenty to occupy yourself with while you settle back into the community. You don't have the time to cart us across the country for who knows how long."

Jesse ignored the protest. "I didn't say I wouldn't either. Where would you be going?"

Lily stepped closer. "We know who brought Annie as a baby to Mamm and Daett. Her name is Olivia Raber, and she's a midwife in Pennsylvania. We want to start there and follow the trail to its end. You know the ways of the English world, and you have an automobile."

"Not exactly a ringing endorsement," Jesse muttered.

Annie wrung her hands. "We shouldn't have come and put you in this position. No one will think ill of you if you turn us down. Just say so."

"It's okay, Annie." He smiled. "I find this interesting, to say the least. How much time do I have before you need an answer?"

"As much time as it takes," Lily said. "We want you to help us. Please."

He pondered for a moment.

Annie burst out again, "I am sorry for the presumption. I can only imagine how this must appear to you, and how bold and forward we seem. If I wasn't desperate, I wouldn't have dared come."

"It's okay," he said again. "My grandparents live in Pennsylvania. We can use that as our base of operations. I'll do it."

"You will?" Lily appeared ecstatic. "Thank you so much!"

Tears glistened in Annie's eyes. "You didn't have to, Jesse. This is so kind of you."

"Don't mention it," he assured her.

He wanted to wipe away her tears, but that would have been most inappropriate.

"Thank you again," Lily gushed, and the two girls climbed back into the buggy. He helped them turn their buggy around and waved as they drove out of the lane.

What have I gotten myself into?

5

A week later, the blaze of the sunrise sent streaks of orange and yellow high into the morning sky. The sheen of low clouds that crisscrossed the horizon added their own texture of deeper reds and blues. Annie sat in the back seat of Jesse's Malibu Classic, with Lily seated in the front. Interstate 80 stretched into the distance in front of them, disappearing into the brightness of the sky's display.

Lily turned around to give her sister a warm smile. "The Lord is with us, Annie. The beauty in the sky this morning is a sign for sure."

"You think?" Annie trembled.

She had so looked forward to this day, but they were setting out on a journey with no certainties. Jesse's steady presence was the only stable force at the moment. The comfort he exuded seemed to fill the whole car. No wonder Lily had fallen in love with the man in her school years.

Jesse sent a quick glance and smile over his shoulder. "We should be at my cousins' place near Goshen by this evening."

"You are so kind to take me on this journey," Annie whispered. "I know I've said it before, but I am grateful. Very grateful!"

"The pleasure is all mine," he responded, clearly focused on the road.

Obviously Jesse didn't think the glorious sunrise a sign from the Lord. Jesse had been out in the English world for three years. He knew things they didn't. They were naïve, homebound women. To set out on a trip like this with the minimal information they had was foolhardy, yet Jesse was taking them out of the kindness of his heart—and perhaps feelings for Lily. She was exactly the kind of woman Jesse needed to settle down in the community. Maybe this journey would be Jesse's payback to Lily for the years he had failed to return her affections. Lily might have jumped at his overtures without any incentive, but she wouldn't forget the gesture either. Jesse was a wise man who knew how to touch a woman's heart.

Jesse turned his head again, and Annie pasted on a quick smile.

"We can stop if either of you wish." He motioned toward a rest stop sign that they were approaching rapidly. "Stretch our legs and get a better view of the sunrise. Looks like we can still enjoy most of the color for a few more minutes. Good timing, I would say." Jesse might not see a sign in the sunrise, but he could appreciate the beauty. Not every man was like that.

"You needn't worry about me," Annie said.

"I think we'll still catch the colors at their peak," Lily gushed from the front seat. "What a splendid idea, Jesse."

"Just me being me," Jesse teased, and Lily made a face at him.

Jesse pulled off the interstate and brought the car to a stop so the three could climb out. A few trees impeded the view, so Jesse led them across the lawn to where the horizon opened in front of them. Lily stood close to him, drinking in the sight.

"Beautiful, isn't it?" Jesse turned to include Annie.

"It is," Annie agreed. She moved closer.

"The Lord made the heavens and the earth in six days," Jesse mused. "Yet He allows His sunrise to hang in the skies long enough for us to enjoy. Wonder why He had no time to savor the progress of His work?"

"Maybe He's letting us enjoy what He didn't," Lily ventured. "You're not doubting the Lord's work, are you?"

Jesse chuckled. "You're wondering if my time away from home cut into my faith?"

"Well, did it?" Lily didn't hide her concern.

Jesse smiled at her. "I don't doubt the Lord making everything out of nothing. I also don't doubt that He took His time and enjoyed Himself."

"Took his time? The Lord called His work goot after He spoke it into existence in six days. That's not very long. Do you believe He took longer than that?" Lily's hand flailed in the air.

Jesse's eyes twinkled. "Am I spoiling the moment?"

"I just wish you wouldn't say things like that," Lily retorted. "I'll be back." She whirled about and made for the restrooms across the lawn.

Jesse's gaze followed her.

"She didn't mean that the way it sounded," Annie whispered.

His smile was soft. "I'm afraid she did, but I'm not offended. I should think twice before I speak. I have been away from the community for three years. I'm a little out of touch."

"You don't have to make excuses. You said nothing wrong."

"Thank you," he said, but his gaze was still on Lily's retreating form. "Maybe we should also use the facilities, then get on the road again." He didn't wait for an answer before he headed across the lawn.

Annie waited a moment longer, turning to look at the dissipating colors in the sky. A sigh slipped from her lips. She would believe that the Lord had painted a sign in the sky this morning for their encouragement. Once on the road again, Lily would settle her quarrel with Jesse. Life in the community taught a simple faith and a trusting heart. She had to believe in the Lord's guiding hand. How else would she have the courage to continue this difficult and perhaps impossible journey?

"Thank You, Lord." Annie sent her prayer toward heaven. "And please be with us the rest of the way."

Minutes later, with the steady rumble of the highway under them, Lily made herself comfortable in the front seat of Jesse's Malibu.

"I see your goot spirits are recovered," Jesse observed. "Sorry about our disagreement."

"You spoke nothing but your heart, and I can respect that."

She couldn't look at him right now. The pain was too much. His words had exposed the gulf that existed between them. Jesse had been out in the world, while she had spent her time in the community. Nothing could be done about that.

"Are you thinking I should confess my erring beliefs to Deacon Bontrager once we get back?" The teasing was still in Jesse's voice.

She almost snapped at him. How could he joke about something so serious?

Annie spoke up from the back seat. "I'd like to hear more of what Jesse was saying, if you don't mind, Lily. I know they might be strange beliefs to the ears of the community, but Jesse seems to believe them."

"That's perfectly okay." Lily forced a smile. "Sorry for my attitude."

"Your reaction was understandable," Jesse told her. "We will talk no more about any of this."

"But Annie wants to hear, and I won't get upset this time," Lily assured him. "I promise. We shouldn't be quarreling anyway."

"I suppose not." Jesse nodded. "But matters of faith can provoke deep feelings."

"Like wanting to find your real Mamm?" Annie asked.

"That's also faith." Jesse turned his head to smile. "Don't you think so, Lily?"

"On that I do agree."

Jesse grinned. "At long last we are on the same page."

Lily forced herself to join in their laughter. Would the day ever come when they would walk together, heart to heart and seeing eye to eye? That day was supposed to have arrived when he returned to the community.

"Is this unity not wunderbah?" Jesse was looking at her.

Lily didn't meet his gaze. "You should tell Annie about your strange beliefs that the Lord didn't create the world in six days."

Jesse paused for a moment. "The truth is I do believe that the Lord made the world in six days, just not that those days were twenty-four-hour days. They were more like long spans of time. I really believe the Lord took His time and carefully made what He made. Is that not how He works in our lives?"

"You do need to speak with Deacon Bontrager," Lily muttered.

Jesse chuckled.

"I'm sorry," Lily said. "I know, I promised."

"What is wrong with that belief?" Annie asked.

"Because a day is a day, and an hour is an hour!" Lily retorted. "How could a day be anything but a day?"

Jesse looked at her with raised eyebrows.

"Well, explain yourself!"

"I'm trying to, and you keep interrupting."

"I can't help myself. You'll have to deal with that."

"Okay." His smile was broad.

At least he found her amusing. Was that not an improvement from the lack of any attention? And Jesse was sitting in the car seat next to her.

"I just think the Lord took more time to make things than we have been told," Jesse continued. "A day with the Lord is like a thousand years. Doesn't the Bible say that as well? He doesn't think of time like we do. I mean, if the Lord simply spoke and there was the earth, why doesn't He speak and there is Annie's Mamm? Instead we have to search for her, and we don't even know what the end of the journey will be.

If we find her, it will be in the Lord's time."

Lily opened and closed her mouth several times before a sound came out. "So you don't think the Lord knew what He was creating before He created?"

"Creating is making something step-by-step," he said. "I think the Lord knew what He was doing, but bringing that idea into reality took some time. He was working with mud and clay, after all."

Lily stilled the sharp intake of her breath. "You should never have left the community. This is what comes from doing your Rumspringa in other lands."

Jesse chuckled. "I doubt if northern Indiana qualifies as 'other lands.' We'll be there by dark and you can see for yourself. There's quite a large Amish community in the vicinity, and they are like us. We are staying with my cousins."

"You heard this belief from them, then?"

"Not directly from them, but from their community."

She had already said too much. *Why can't I just be quiet?* Her relationship with Jesse seemed to be doomed at every turn.

Annie spoke up. "I like the idea of the Lord working with us frail and weak creatures like He always has. That thought comforts me. The Lord knows I want to find my Mamm, and He's leading us there, bringing into being the things in our hearts that should be there, shaped by His own hand."

Jesse was grinning from ear to ear. "That's exactly what I'm talking about. The application is perfect."

Jesse had never called anything Lily had done or said perfect. Not the pictures she used to draw in school and leave lying where Jesse would see them. Not one of the smiles she had invested in the man. Yet now something her sister had said was perfect to him. She couldn't deny that it stung.

"I'm glad your thoughts are inspiring someone." Lily finally found her voice, but the words had a bite to them.

Jesse's grin didn't fade. "You'd like them too if you'd open your heart, Lily."

"Maybe," she allowed.

Jesse hadn't rejected her yet, and he still smiled. Lily chatted lightly about the passing scenery for the rest of the miles they traveled that day, and Jesse seemed happy with her efforts.

They arrived at his cousins' home soon after the sun had set, as Jesse had predicted. The young Amish couple were pleasant, and after a brief visit on the couch, they ushered the weary travelers to their upstairs rooms.

Lily kept the cheerfulness in her voice once the bedroom door was closed. "So far, so goot, Annie, don't you think?"

Annie appeared weary and exhausted but still smiled. "Yah, I agree. I have much to be thankful for."

Lily cracked open the bedroom door to peer into the hallway. Jesse had vanished from sight and the light under his door had gone out. He must have fallen asleep the moment his head hit the pillow.

"You are goot together," Annie said encouragingly when Lily shut the door again.

Lily didn't answer. What was there to say? She changed into her nightclothes by the light of the flickering kerosene lamp and slipped under the heavy quilt to rest her head on the soft goose down pillow with a long sigh.

Sleep didn't come for an hour or so, long after Annie's breathing had deepened in the bed across the darkened room.

The following day, Indiana turned into Ohio, and Ohio into Pennsylvania. The GPS claimed the Pennsylvania Turnpike lay ten miles ahead. Jesse squinted at the screen. He was more exhausted than he had been last evening, and he was ready to arrive at his grandparents' place for the night. They had been on the road since four that morning, leaving his cousins' house north of Goshen with a light breakfast and whispered thanks.

At the moment, Lily had her head back on the headrest, apparently asleep. Annie was in the back seat again and hadn't spoken in the last hour. They were talked out, he supposed. Jesse flicked through the radio's music stations. Country was his favorite genre, but he had played Christian stations the last two days when he could find them. Otherwise, he kept the radio turned off. Lily and Annie had long ago left their Rumspringas behind them. He should not tempt them.

This was his last fling, regardless of how the adventure turned out. After this trip, he would settle down in the community and leave the English world behind him. Jesse's glance lingered on Lily's sleeping face. The girl was a natural choice for a Frau. Lily had always adored him, and she would serve as a buffer against the liberal ideas he had acquired during his Rumspringa, once more conversations like the one back at the rest area yesterday occurred. He wouldn't be able to keep his thoughts secret. Nor did he want to.

Most of the men in the community would chuckle and consider his observations harmless on how exactly creation occurred. But he would be marked, and that would create questions in some minds. How better to counteract doubts than to have someone like Lily by his side? Deacon Bontrager would be pleased with his choice. Lily could handle herself well with the Scriptures.

A smile crept over Jesse's face. Lily had put forth a fiery resistance to him yesterday. The girl had to know the risk this played with his affections for her, yet Lily had charged forward undeterred. He admired that in a woman—the courage to battle for one's faith, even in the face of loss. But were those feelings enough to build a life together? Would Lily be satisfied once she figured out that his heart wasn't hers?

Jesse made the turn onto the turnpike, slowing to pick up his tollway ticket. Neither girl stirred. Their hosts last night had been accommodating, but they were strangers to Lily and Annie. The girls must have gotten less sleep than he did. He had fallen asleep immediately, exhausted as he was from the long drive.

Tonight would be a repeat at his grandparents' home. Especially after the hearty meal his grandmother would prepare for them.

"You will not eat before you arrive, no matter what hour that is," his grandmother had ordered him, returning his call from the phone shack near their home. "I'll keep supper warm in the oven."

There would be mashed potatoes and gravy, with steaks for the meat dish if he knew Grandma. No expense would be spared for their arrival. Jesse's parents' move to the distant community in Nebraska had not been welcomed, so homecomings were treasured and each moment cherished. This was part of what pulled him home from his life with the English, where there was a fragmentation in the broader culture, one that did not exist in Amish life.

He should thank Lily that she was willing to love him even with the strange ideas he had acquired while on Rumspringa. Instead he had found Annie fascinating. She had liked his ideas. They were alike in so many ways. Displaced, seeking to find their way back through unknown lands. That was dangerous, and he had planned to leave risk behind him.

Jesse craned his neck for a peek into the back seat. Annie had awakened, and her smile warmed his heart.

6

Annie awoke with a start in the predawn darkness. She climbed out of bed to light the kerosene lamp and dress by the dim glow. Lily, asleep in the bed beside her, did not awaken. Her sister must be exhausted from the long drive yesterday, coupled with the hearty supper Grandma Yoder had prepared for them when Jesse pulled into the driveway a little before seven.

With the kerosene lamp in one hand, Annie cracked open the bedroom door and glanced out before she tiptoed into the hallway. Faint noises came from the kitchen downstairs, so Grandma Yoder was up, preparing another meal for her beloved grandson. Jesse had a lot of people who held him close to their hearts—first in Indiana, where Jesse's cousins had welcomed them for the night, now in far-flung Lancaster County, the place Annie herself had left as an infant.

Annie clung to the handrail to steady herself while the shadows from thc flickering flame danced on the dark walls. Jesse's room was at the other end of the hall, the thin space under the door dark. She was the only one who was up other than Grandma Yoder. Her heart was restless, wondering what the future held, thinking about what lay ahead of them: the search, the questions, the empty spaces without answers. Through the night she had tossed and turned, falling asleep for a few precious hours before awakening again with such abruptness.

The steps squeaked as Annie descended, the sound familiar from the old farmhouse at home. She was far from Nebraska but still among her people. She would have to remind herself often of this truth when she didn't know what lay ahead. She would always be what she was now. That would not change, regardless of what she might find on this search.

Annie stepped out of the stairwell and peeked around the corner. Grandma Yoder's smiling face greeted her. "I thought I heard someone coming."

Bacon and ham lay on the countertop, surrounded by egg and oatmeal cartons.

"Can I help you?" Annie set the lamp on the kitchen table.

"You are a guest. You should rest!" Grandma Yoder exclaimed. "And after traveling such long hours yesterday. I can't imagine doing that at my age."

Annie made a face. "I'm not used to it either, but I am thankful. Jesse brought us out here when he didn't have to."

"That's Jesse for you." Grandma Yoder's face glowed. "He's such a special visitor, and so are you girls. I am honored."

Annie smiled. "That is kind of you to say. I have to admit that Lily was the one with the courage to ask him, but Jesse didn't hesitate."

"I'm sure Jesse would have brought you even if you had been the one doing the asking," Grandma Yoder assured her.

Annie began to heat a pan over the stove, then dropped in the thick strips of bacon despite Grandma Yoder's earlier objections.

"Are they dating?" Grandma Yoder raised her eyebrows. "Lily and Jesse?"

Annie winced. "My sister would take Jesse at the drop of a hat, but Jesse never returned Lily's feelings. The truth is, they are well suited."

Grandma Yoder's eyebrows were still up.

"Oh, they are!" Annie insisted.

Heat crept up her neck, but she hoped Grandma Yoder would attribute the cause to the hot stove.

"Just don't ignore the Lord's ways, child," Grandma Yoder chided. "And keep your heart open."

"But I . . . we . . . ," Annie sputtered. Finally she settled on something to say. "I'm going in one direction, and Jesse is heading back to the community in Nebraska to settle down. He's only helping us out and will doubtlessly sell his car once we—I mean, once he gets back."

"You're not going back? After you've found your Mamm?"

"I have to find her first," Annie fudged.

"You'll find her." Grandma Yoder sounded quite confident. "The heart always leads you home, and afterward your heart will take you back to the community. You are already there, Annie, and your affection for Jesse shows on your face when you look at him."

"Now you have embarrassed me!" Annie exclaimed, covering her face with her apron. "I'm not stealing a boyfriend from my sister, and besides, I'm not what Jesse needs."

"I don't think you call this stealing," Grandma Yoder corrected her gently. "And perhaps Jesse should decide what he needs, providing you agree, of course."

"I . . . can we talk about something else?"

Grandma Yoder patted Annie on the arm. "I'm sorry. I'm pushy this morning, and to my wunderbah guest at that. I will quit now, so you can enjoy your brief stay in our home. You're headed up to see the midwife Olivia Raber today, right?"

Annie turned the bacon over, the sizzle filling the small kitchen. "That's our plan. Do you think she'll speak with us?"

Grandma Yoder shrugged. "Olivia will talk with you. How much information she will give you, I don't know. Enough, I hope, to continue your search. The woman knows all the secrets of the community, I'm afraid."

Annie groaned. "I thought you were so positive and sure only a moment ago that I would find my Mamm."

Grandma Yoder's response was cut off when Lily rushed into the kitchen. "Why did no one call me? This is so embarrassing."

"You needed your sleep, dear," Grandma Yoder said. "But there's still plenty to be done, seeing how you girls insist on helping."

"We certainly do!" Lily declared. "Where can I help? The oatmeal? Eggs?"

"The oatmeal," Grandma Yoder told her, and Lily headed for the sink to fill the pan with water.

"So what do you do back home?" Grandma Yoder inquired.

While their hostess made small talk with Lily, Annie mulled over their conversation from a few moments before. Was she to open her heart to Jesse while she searched for her English Mamm? The two goals seemed exclusionary. Her heart couldn't handle the pain of double failure, not at the same time. And what about Lily? No, it was better to stay focused and let the days unfold on their own.

Annie's thoughts refocused when loud thumps and bangs came from the washroom just outside the kitchen walls. Seconds later the door swung open and Grandpa Yoder's hearty "Goot morning, everyone!" echoed in the small room. "I see you girls have breakfast about ready, but where is that lazy grandson of mine?"

They all joined in the laughter. Grandpa Yoder settled into a kitchen chair with a sigh. "It's great that Jesse brought both of you all the way here from Nebraska. It's not often that we have two such beautiful visitors in our humble abode at the same time."

"We're glad we're here," Annie assured him with a smile.

Jesse's sleepy face appeared in the kitchen doorway. "What's all the noise about?"

"Sit down and get ready for this wunderbah breakfast the womenfolk are cooking up," Grandpa Yoder ordered. "It's about time you got up. The day is a-wasting."

Jesse moaned and sat down as laughter filled the kitchen again.

An hour later, Annie led the way up the wooden sidewalk, stepping high to avoid the fresh shoots that stretched skyward through the rotting boards. Both Lily and Jesse, walking behind her, were doing the same. The place was a dump. Olivia Raber might be Lancaster County's best midwife, but she didn't keep her place up to par with the other Amish farms. A goat was tethered near the front porch with a rope around its neck. This was obviously the Olivia Raber version of a lawn mower.

"You don't see that every day," Jesse muttered. "Especially in Lancaster County."

"Takes all kinds," Lily replied. "Smile. We need the woman in a goot mood."

"I am smiling," he retorted. "Is the goat smiling? That's what I want to know. He's looking at me funny."

Lily giggled. "He has horns, but you can handle him. You are an Amish farm boy."

Jesse raised an eyebrow at her. "Says the woman who is hiding behind me."

"The thing looks fierce." Lily stepped so that Jesse was fully between her and the goat.

Annie hadn't paused, striding forward while the goat regarded her with a tilted head.

"See?" Jesse said. "That is courage."

"Annie has more at stake in this than you and I do. But that's still no excuse." Lily moved out from behind him and headed toward the door.

Jesse outpaced Lily as they followed Annie up the porch steps. The front door opened before they arrived.

"Who might you be?" asked an old Amish woman with a deeply wrinkled face.

Obviously, this must be Olivia Raber.

Jesse stepped forward. "This is Annie and Lily Miller from Nebraska. I'm Jesse Yoder, also from there . . . well, originally. My grandparents live—"

"I know your grandparents," Olivia interrupted. "Why are you here?" Olivia's gaze swept over Annie to linger on Lily. "Your Frau doesn't seem to be expecting."

"Ah, no, we aren't wed," Jesse stumbled. "I mean, Lily isn't expecting and neither is Annie. We are here for another matter."

"Why are you here?" Olivia peered at him. "That's the question."

Lily hid her red face. The midwife thought she was Jesse's Frau!

"I want to learn who my birth Mamm is," Annie spoke up. "My parents told me you brought me to them when I was a baby."

"Did they now?" Olivia's gaze shifted to Annie. "I thought people kept such things secret, but the times are changing apparently." Olivia held open the door. "You might as well come in. I don't discuss such things on my front porch."

They were soon seated on the couch, and Olivia faced them on a chair she had pulled in from somewhere.

"Thank you for making time for us," Annie offered.

Olivia ignored the comment. "So what is this about me bringing you to your Mamm and Daett? Tell me what you know."

Lily listened as Annie recounted the familiar tale. The information was sparse and seemed even more so when the words were spoken out loud. Olivia could refuse to say a thing, and they would have no further recourse.

Apparently the same thought occurred to Olivia. "Maybe this had best be allowed to sleep in peace," the woman suggested. "You have a goot home with the Millers. You are loved and respected in the community. Is this not so?"

"Yah," Annie agreed.

Olivia nodded. "These are things of the heart, and the heart is easily injured. My advice is that you go back home and leave this alone. You can always tell yourself you tried, but don't frustrate yourself, Annie. There is no goot end to this road. Believe me. I'm an old woman, and I know."

"But I must find my English Mamm," Annie insisted. "For years my heart has yearned to know who my real Mamm is and to meet her."

"I couldn't tell you that, even if I knew," Olivia said. "Which I don't."

"But you know something—you must." Annie's voice was desperate. "A baby doesn't come from nowhere, dropped from the sky."

Olivia's chuckle was dry. "Yah, I know that. Men sin and the women bear the sorrow. That's how it goes, for the goot and for the bad."

"You must tell her what you know." Lily couldn't keep the words back.

Olivia's gaze shifted to her. "And why do I have to do that?"

"Because I have seen my sister wait for this hour. Annie has wanted to meet her English Mamm since I can remember. Now we are here. If you don't tell Annie what she needs to know, we will always remember that you could have and decided not to. You will be to blame—"

Olivia stopped Lily with an upraised hand. "Guilt doesn't work for me, dear. You were doing much better before that. I understand youth and their dreams. The tender touch of the Lord's hand they are, melting soon enough before the harsh realities of the world. But who am I to question the Almighty's ways, who gives anew to each generation the hopes that die in the hearts of the one gone before? So, fine. I will tell some of what I know, but do not ask me for more. Agreed?"

Annie had paled, and her only answer was a quick nod.

"There is a crisis pregnancy center in Lancaster, the Hope Clinic. An Amish couple I shall not name volunteered their time there and brought you to me along with your sister."

"My sister!" Annie gasped, now completely white.

Olivia ignored the outburst. "Your twin sister. This Amish couple acted on the instructions of your mother. You were both to be placed in Amish homes. I know not why. I took the couple at their word and found a place for you with the childless young Miller couple, your Mamm and Daett, and your twin with someone else. The Hope Clinic notified the state, and you were both legally adopted."

"My twin and my Mamm." Annie trembled. "Is either of them in the community? Can—"

"I don't know child, and I couldn't tell you if they were," Olivia interrupted again. "You will have to take things from there, Annie. And now I have to go. Wendell Chupp's Frau, Sarah, needs my attentions. She has an appointment with me in an hour, for her firstborn. The baby was breeched last week and due in two. You can pray, if you think of her."

"We will," Annie assured her as they were ushered out the door.

Lily hung back to ask, "Are you sure there is no more you can tell us?"

"Out!" Olivia ordered, and she closed the door in their faces.

Down at the end of the wooden sidewalk, Jesse opened the car door for Annie while Lily walked around the other side to climb in. He offered his hand until Annie was seated. The girl was still white as a sheet.

Jesse climbed behind the wheel. "We should pray." He didn't wait for an answer, but began to speak: "Our Father, Who art in heaven, look down upon us this moment and comfort our hearts. Give us courage and wisdom as we proceed with the information You have so graciously given us. Comfort also Sarah Chupp's heart, as she faces the birth of a child for the first time. Amen."

Lily looked strangely at him. "Are you a preacher or something?"

"No. Why?"

"You prayed out loud."

"What is wrong with that?"

"Nothing, I guess. But no one really does that back in the community, not unless—"

He grunted. "Be that as it may, I learned to pray in my struggles while I was away from home, so you'll just have to accept that. Okay?"

"I'm sorry," Lily whispered. "And you do pray well."

"Goot to hear." His dark look disappeared, and he turned to Annie. "Are you all right? That must have been quite a shock."

The answer was a muffled sob as she continued to stare out the car window.

"This is goot news, Annie," he said comfortingly, "and a decent start. We know more now than we did before, and we'll track down this lead at the Hope Clinic. Somehow we'll figure out where your Mamm and your sister are."

Annie's smile was thin through her tears. He wanted to gather her up in his arms and kiss her cheeks dry, but there was the seat back between them, and Lily was in the car even if Annie would accept his comfort.

"Everything will work out," he told her.

Jesse started the Malibu and drove out of the lane, while Olivia's goat followed their every move with a baleful stare.

7

As the Malibu crept along in the morning traffic toward the town of Lancaster, Annie clutched the armrest in the back seat. She had a twin sister? Her whole body was still numb. How was she to deal with that? Now she had to find two people instead of one? Through the long evening, and even in her dreams, the questions had raced through her head.

Annie pressed her fingers against her forehead. In the front seat, Lily kept up a steady chatter. "The roads are so densely populated. The shops are everywhere, and look at their gardens, Jesse. They make mine look like a weed patch."

"Your garden back in Nebraska looked fine to me," Jesse said warmly.

"You haven't seen it, and if you have, you don't look at gardens like I do."

Lily hadn't been silent since they'd left Jesse's grandparents' home thirty minutes ago. Grandma Yoder had served them a hearty breakfast of bacon, eggs, oatmeal, and pancakes.

"Take your time and eat your fill," Grandma Yoder had insisted. "You'll need your strength for the day's journey. Plus, I treasure every moment you are here in our home. We are so happy to have our grandson and his friends with us." Her smile had lit up the whole kitchen.

Jesse came from a solid family with deep roots in the Amish community—unlike Annie. She had an English Mamm. Jesse had returned from his Rumspringa, called home by the voices from the past, including Lily. Her sister had loved the man long before Jesse left

Nebraska. Jesse had remembered and returned to find what was missing in his life. Lily would make exactly the kind of Frau he needed. Lily was Amish to the core, stable, funny, and came from an impeccable lineage. Even in her brief Rumspringa in Nebraska, Lily had never strayed far from home.

Clearly oblivious to Annie's thoughts, Lily chattered away. "Even with their nice places and gardens, can you imagine living here with these tourists? They must be underfoot night and day. And look how they stare."

"I know," Jesse chuckled. "Makes you appreciate the quiet, open fields of home."

"And look around!" Lily peered out of the car window. "Buggies, cars, and shops all mixed together. We haven't traveled twenty miles from your grandparents' place, and it's taken over half an hour."

"I can take you back to Nebraska," Jesse teased.

"I'm not that homesick, and we have to find Annie's Mamm and sister." Lily turned in her seat. "How are you doing, Annie? We haven't heard a peep out of you since we left the house."

"Just thinking." Annie blinked back a tear. "Wondering what we will find today."

"I can only imagine. But just think—this may be the end of your journey. How many years have you longed for this moment? Ever since I can remember."

"We may not find the final answer today," Jesse suggested gently. "These things sometimes take a little time."

Lily silenced him with a glare. "Don't be throwing cold water on our venture. The Lord is blessing us. Let us not despair. We will find Annie's Mamm and be on our way home the day after tomorrow."

Jesse smiled. "To a great morning then, and to the Lord's blessings."

Annie kept quiet. Jesse understood better than Lily did that even if she found her Mamm today, that would not be the end of the journey. In a way, success would be the beginning. Maybe she could stay in Lancaster County, and Lily could return to Nebraska with Jesse. But that might not be decent—Lily traveling alone with Jesse. She would have to make the trip back home with her and return later to face difficult decisions. Would she join her Mamm in the English world, or stay in the community? Would peace come either way? Would she finally know if she could be an Amish woman, even if she had an English Mamm?

Jesse slowed his Malibu as they approached the town. Lily was busy with the map in her lap.

"Turn left ahead. Two streets down."

Jesse kept a smile on his face and did as he was told. The two were functioning as a happy Amish couple. Annie swallowed hard. Here she was, on the cusp of finding a missing link to her real Mamm, and overcome at the same time with sorrow for what could have been. What if she had been born Amish? Would Jesse look at her differently? Might she have looked at Jesse with interest years ago? If that had been the case, she might have been the one riding in the front seat instead of Lily.

"Here we are!" Lily sang out.

"The Hope Clinic. Still the same name," Jesse observed. "That makes things easier."

Lily turned to peer at Annie. "Are you still okay?"

Annie nodded and tried to smile. Lily clearly wasn't convinced and hopped out to open the car door for her. Jesse hovered in the background. He appeared ready to offer his arm for the walk to the front door but must have changed his mind.

"Are we ready?" Jesse asked instead.

Annie gathered herself. "I am. Please help us, Lord."

"Amen," Jesse and Lily said in unison.

Annie headed up the walkway while Jesse hurried ahead to open the door of the clinic. Here she was, in tears on this special morning. Her heart was pulled both forward and backward, between the home she had grown up in and now the home that must lie out there with the woman who was her real Mamm.

Lily held Annie's arm and led her through the clinic door.

"Can I help you?" the young girl behind the desk asked.

"Uh . . . ah . . . ," Annie began, then looked helplessly at her sister.

Lily stepped closer. "Goot morning. I am Lily Miller, and this is my sister, Annie. Could we speak with the person in charge of the clinic?"

The young girl appeared confused. "I can handle your medical information here at the front desk." She pushed a clipboard of papers across the desk. "Which one of you is expecting? Or are you both?"

Lily's face flushed. "No. I mean, it's not that."

"We are here about my adoption," Annie managed, her voice a whisper. "We believe the clinic was involved when I was a baby."

"Ah, just a minute." The young woman scurried toward a back room and closed the door behind her.

Lily didn't dare glance at Jesse's face. How embarrassing this was, twice now, but the misunderstandings had been natural ones.

"We are going to have to be firm when she comes back," Jesse said, and Lily drew a deep breath. Jesse understood.

"I don't know if I can be firm," Annie said faintly. "I'm still light-headed. I thought I was going to faint a moment ago."

"Then we will be firm for you." Jesse reached for Annie's hand, and she leaned on him for support. Jesse had never offered to hold

Lily's hand on the long drive from Nebraska, but she should not begrudge Annie the comfort of Jesse's strength. This was a man's normal reaction to a woman in need. Jesse meant nothing special by the gesture, she was sure. The two appeared perfectly natural as they waited in front of the desk, and a little color had returned to Annie's cheeks.

The door opened and the young woman returned with a kind-looking older man, who extended his hand. "Dr. Ezra Meitner. And you are Lily and Annie."

Lily shook his hand. "I hope you can answer my sister's questions. We have come a long way searching for answers."

"From Nebraska," Jesse added, still holding Annie's hand.

"I see." Ezra's glance took in the three of them. "Something about an adoption. Perhaps we should step into my office."

Dr. Meitner retreated and they followed. He offered them chairs in a semicircle in front of his small desk. "Please be seated." His hand took in the room with a flourish. "We make the needs of our clients a priority. This isn't much, but we can talk here in private."

Jesse gave the doctor a kind smile. "We are grateful for the work you do here and for the work of the clinic in the past. That is why we're here. Annie was adopted through an Amish couple who used to volunteer their help, and perhaps still do. We're a little short on information, but we hoped it would be enough to begin."

"Well." The doctor's face wrinkled apologetically. "Those are confidential subjects, so obviously that's why the information is scanty. Are you sure this clinic was involved in Annie's adoption? We rarely facilitate those but simply refer the parents to the proper agencies."

"We are sure the clinic was involved through the Amish couple," Jesse said. "So there have to be records of who the mother was and who the adoptive parents were."

"I'm sorry." Dr. Meitner's face wrinkled even further. "Surely you know we can't disclose such matters. There are strict laws that govern adoptions."

"There has to be some way," Jesse insisted. "Annie's search has brought her to your door. If a young girl wants to find her mother, surely she has the right to do that. Perhaps you can give us the name of someone who is not under the scrutiny of the state."

"You're asking a lot, young man." Dr. Meitner made an attempt at a smile. "We really can't give out information, but if you want, you can visit Wanda Coleman, who lives here in town. She's the daughter of our former director, Mrs. Leslie. Perhaps there is a journal Mrs. Leslie kept in her personal effects, or something Mrs. Leslie might have dropped in conversation with her daughter. There would be no names, but events might be reconstructed if the daughter has the details from you. Don't expect much. A lot of women go through the clinic, and you are grasping at straws."

"Is there a legal way in which information can be obtained?" Jesse asked.

Dr. Meitner stood. "If you can obtain a court subpoena, we would certainly comply. I'm not trying to be difficult. I really do sympathize with your plight, but like I said, it's the law. We cannot disclose that kind of information without a legal order."

"And the likelihood of that?"

"Slim at best, and it would be a long process. I'm sorry. I really am."

Dr. Meitner clearly wanted this session to end. Annie had tears on her cheeks. They did nothing to convince the doctor, but he was not being cruel. The rules were the rules.

"We should be going then," Jesse said.

Dr. Meitner scribbled an address on a piece of paper and handed it to Jesse. The young girl at the desk gave them a nervous smile as the doctor led the way out of the office.

Once in the car, Jesse handed the slip of paper to Lily with a grim face. Lily found the address on the city map. A few turns later and a mile farther into town, they pulled up in front of a small brick bungalow.

"To better success this time!" Jesse proclaimed as he climbed out to open Annie's door. He held Annie's hand for the short walk up to the front door.

Lily hurried ahead and knocked. When a woman opened the door, Lily said, "Excuse us, please. We're looking for Wanda Coleman, the daughter of Mrs. Leslie, the former director at the Hope Clinic."

"That would be me." A smile spread across Wanda's face. "How can I help you?"

The introductions were made and the story spilled out quickly.

"Do come in," Wanda told them. "I don't know if I can help, as my mother didn't keep journals that I know of, but you should sit down while we talk this through."

"So there are no journals?" Jesse asked as they followed the woman inside. "Why would Dr. Meitner mention that?"

"I don't know." Wanda laughed. "Mom wasn't a secretive person, but I guess that impression could be gathered from the work she did. Or maybe Dr. Meitner could imagine her keeping a journal."

"He was just trying to help," Annie said to Jesse. "He has a kind heart. I could see that right away."

"That he does." Wanda showed them to chairs. "I could place a personal plea with Dr. Meitner, but from my experience with Mom, no one talks for fear the state would come down on them. Hope Clinic is monitored closely because of the work they do. They are a medical facility after all."

"So the court option is our only course." Annie's face had paled. "But that could take weeks, and what would the community say about my appealing to an English court? I've already pushed this far enough with my journey to Pennsylvania."

"You can pray, I guess. In fact, let's pray right now." Wanda didn't wait for agreement but bowed her head. "Dear Father in heaven, Who loves us the deepest, You have placed the cry for family and home in our hearts, bend low over the hurt in Annie's heart, and answer with Your divine strength. Open doors that are closed, and lead Annie to the desire of her heart. Amen."

"Amen," Jesse echoed. "Thank you for that."

They stood. Annie opened her arms and embraced Wanda. "You'll never know how much those words mean to me."

"May you find the answers you seek," Wanda said, and the two clung to each other for a long time.

"You okay?" Jesse asked, and he reached over to squeeze Lily's hand.

She nodded but couldn't meet his gaze.

An hour later, Jesse parked the Malibu beside his grandparents' barn and rested his head on the steering wheel. Little had been said on the drive back to the farm, with each of them lost in their thoughts. They had not yet found the next turn in the road, but somewhere there was direction. He couldn't accept anything else. Not after the long journey Annie had traveled to get to this point. They couldn't return to the community empty-handed.

Grandpa Yoder appeared in the barn door, and he walked over to stand by the car. "No goot news from the glum faces, I'm thinking."

"You could say that." Jesse ran through a brief summary of the day.

"The Lord's heart is toward the widows and the orphans," Grandpa Yoder said. "I know that Annie isn't an orphan, but she was abandoned once. I think the Lord will answer somehow."

"Any suggestions?" Jesse glanced up at his grandfather's face.

"I don't know. Let's go talk to your grandmother. She's the wise one."

Jesse chuckled as he climbed out of the car. Grandpa wanted

someone to second his opinion, whatever that was.

"You think he has an idea?" Annie whispered when he opened the car door for her.

Jesse smiled. "Grandpa wouldn't want us to speak with Grandma if he didn't."

Grandpa led them up the walk. Lily followed behind Annie and Jesse, who glanced over his shoulder to give her a smile. "You were a great help today with everything."

"Thank you," Lily said, but there was concern in her eyes. Maybe that was because of the hard day, but he expected the reason went deeper. Lily was a wonderful woman, but he had never been able to open his heart to her. This trip hadn't changed his feelings yet.

Grandpa held open the door for them, and they spilled inside. "Grandma!" he hollered. "Come here for a moment."

There was rustling upstairs and Grandma appeared with her cleaning broom and dustpan. "How did everything go today? Goot, I hope." A tentative smile flickered on her face.

Grandpa filled her in and her smile vanished. "Do you think the next step would be to visit Mose and Susie Wagler?" he said. "I'm thinking they are the ones who used to volunteer their time at the Hope Clinic."

"That's exactly what they should do!" Grandma agreed. "Mose and Susie are the only people I can remember doing such a thing. I'm sure they will have something to say that will help, so enough of the down faces. I will feed you supper, and after a goot night's sleep, the Lord will continue to show the way."

"That's how I feel," Grandpa agreed.

"I hope you are right," Annie whispered. "Thank you so very much—however this turns out."

"It will be okay," Jesse assured her, but the fear still showed in Annie's eyes when he let go of her hand.

8

In the middle of the night, the moonlight flooded through the open upstairs bedroom window of Grandpa Yoder's old farmhouse and danced off the dark hardwood floors. Annie tossed under the thick quilt, her dreams tormented. In them she stretched for the sky as she ran across the open fields with the night sky above her head. She was chilled to the bone. Dawn was hours away, so why was she outside? And where was the house of Jesse's grandparents with her warm bed? She had to find something, but what? Her Mamm, and now her sister? The impossible seemed within her grasp. Hope began to throb in her heart, but then she stumbled and sprawled on the ground.

"We love you, Annie," voices whispered in the distance. "We have always loved you."

"Mamm? Sister?" Annie rose and ran toward the sound. They were out there in the night.

"You're almost here. Reach for us."

She had heard her natural Mamm's voice before, in the beat of her heart, in the agony of the chasm inside her.

"We are meant to be a family. Come!"

Annie hurried on. Tree branches waved in her face and stung her cheeks. The road led downward, through a river with rocks that cut her feet, but she pressed on. She must find them. They were ahead of her, if she could strain high enough, if she could run far enough.

Her breath became ragged, and her lungs burned. What if she stopped? Would she hear them again? Would they be gone when her strength returned?

The silhouettes of the swaying trees were behind her, visible against the brilliant stars. The river was a torrent, the sound of its rushing water filling her ears. She would never be able to cross the water again. She would drown trying, and home lay in that direction. In front of her were open fields with deep shadows in the distance.

She ran again, the chill of the night kept at bay by her exertions. Her dress was soaked to her knees, but she didn't dare stop. She must find them regardless of the cost or the danger. The darkness, the cold, the fear would not turn her back.

Annie moved her lips, but no sound came out. The shadows ahead formed into more woods, fierce and menacing.

"We are in here, Annie. In here!" the voices called again.

The creak of tree limbs moved in sync with the sound. Terror stopped Annie for a moment, but the voices drew her again. She must enter. If she turned back, the years would take their toll, and she would always wonder what lay in the shelter of the forest trees. She must find them!

Annie entered, forcing each foot forward. Her dress caught on a bush and tore as she lunged forward. The limbs of the trees seemed to sigh in the wind as they moved overhead. The moonlight trickled down through the leaves, the beams shattered before they touched the ground. The darkness clutched the light as if to stifle it.

Annie pressed on until the light above her head faded entirely. She had to feel with her fingers to free her dress from nearby trees and branches. The darkness became so complete that it hid her hands even when she held them close to her face. She cried out, yearning for the light long vanished in the groaning treetops. She could not find them.

The voices were silent now. There was nothing here to find.

She stumbled backward, then found herself flailing in open space. Where had this cliff come from? She fell. She would land with a deadly crash. No one could survive this fall.

The quilt flew across the room as Annie jolted awake with a strangled cry. Her arms were soaked with sweat, and her head ached. She had been dreaming. She wasn't outside. The woods and the voices weren't real—or were they?

Annie's feet found the hardwood floor, and she gently laid the quilt back on the bed. She tiptoed to the open window, where a blaze of moonlight streamed in. That part of the dream had been true. The soft breeze stirred Annie's hair and soothed her panic. There were no woods visible in the distance, only the well-tended fields of Lancaster County. She had dreamed everything, or most of it.

Annie slipped on her housecoat. Lily was fast asleep in her bed across the room. If she had cried out in her sleep, Lily had not awakened, but her sister had always been able to sleep through anything. The wooden stairs creaked as she made her way down, but if anyone heard, the sound would be attributed to the night air and its effects on the old wood.

Annie slipped through the front door and closed the latch softly behind her. Her feet were bare, and the moonlight was so bright it seemed fierce.

A sob caught in Annie's throat. The dream had not been real, but the throbbing in her heart was real enough. She had to find them, her Mamm and her twin sister. But how? Every step appeared blocked before she arrived. Had the years of longing, of waiting, of hoping been in vain? Where would this search end—in despair, in hopelessness, in regret? Was she doomed to a life of wondering, always trying to find what was not there, only to be told that yet more lay beyond the horizon?

She had a sister, a twin! Why would no one tell her more?

Annie clung to the split-rail fence that ran along the back of Grandpa Yoder's old farmhouse. Morning would come soon. Would the sun find her still here, lost in a search that went nowhere?

"Annie?" A man's voice caused her to jump. Was she dreaming again? No one could have heard her leave the house.

"Annie!"

She dared look back. Jesse was framed in the doorway of the house, his face alarmed in the light of the moon. His gaze met hers, and he came toward her.

Tears streamed down Annie's face as he approached, barefoot as she was.

"Annie," he repeated, softer now. "Why are you out here?"

The answer was a tortured sob.

He came closer and took her hand. "What is wrong?"

"I was dreaming, looking for them and hearing their voices. I ran in the darkness, through the woods, but I found nothing."

Jesse held out his arms and she nestled against him, his strength a deep comfort, his arms around her a band of protection against the darkness of the imagined woods.

"Would you have come with me?" She looked up at him.

"Come where?"

"Into the dark woods."

His arms tightened. "You don't have to go there. It was a dream."

"But you are coming with me, searching with me, trying to find my missing life."

"Only because you want me to," he said. "I don't find anything missing in you, Annie Miller. You are a wonderful woman, perfect as you are."

"Don't say that!" she cried. "I don't feel whole or perfect."

"That's why we are going to find your Mamm." He held her close and fussed with her loose hair. "Somehow I believe this. I don't know why or how, but the Lord will go with us. I have felt Him with us so far, and that should not change."

"You do?"

"Yah, I do. I'm sorry you were troubled with dreams. Do they happen often?"

"Not really." She laid her head against his chest. "I don't know why I had such a nightmare tonight."

"You are not to blame," he whispered into her hair. "You are not to blame for any of this."

"Oh, Jesse, you say such wonderful things."

He chuckled. "You are wonderful, Annie, not what I say."

She gazed up into his face.

"What?" he asked.

She shook her head. "I just want to forget everything: the nightmare, the woods, the darkness, the—"

"It's okay," he interrupted. "It will all be okay."

Lily awakened from a deep sleep and sat up in bed. What had awakened her? The flood of moonlight revealed an empty bed across the room. Had Annie heard something and gone to investigate? Lily listened in the stillness of the old farmhouse. There was no sound in the distance.

Lily pushed the quilt back and hurried to the open window. Dim forms were outlined along the split-rail fence below, with their hands entwined. Lily stilled the sharp intake of her breath. *Annie and Jesse! Out together! Talking!* Obviously they enjoyed each other's company.

She shouldn't be spying, but this was not intruding. Annie and

Jesse stood in plain sight. What had happened that couldn't wait until morning? Why had they felt the need to leave the house?

Lily leaned closer to the window. Their shoulders were touching now. Had Jesse developed feelings for Annie? Was Jesse making his intentions known to Annie before the two made their affections public? But that was strange. Jesse wasn't like that . . . or was he? Would Jesse ask Annie to meet him outside on a moonlit night to talk of love? Lily wondered if she had ever understood the man she had loved for so long.

Lily pulled back from the window after another quick glance at the forms holding hands beside the fence. She slowly made her way across the hardwood floor. Was this another surprise, another unanticipated turn in the road? So many unexpected things had happened on this journey. Would a blending of Jesse and Annie's hearts be so surprising? Maybe she had always known or at least suspected. Jesse had spent plenty of time comforting Annie in the past few days. Why would he not fall in love with her sister?

Lily sighed and climbed back into bed. She must not hold anything against Annie, even if the scene along the split-rail fence was a lovers' conversation. She had come along on this trip to help Annie find the answers she sought. Now Jesse was obviously part of that. Why should she be angry? If she could not win his heart, then he was fair game.

Lily pulled the quilt up to her chin, her long hair tossed on either side of the pillow. Her heart should throb and ache at this moment, but it didn't. There was regret and sorrow but no tears. Jesse had never loved her. She knew that. The days would go on like they had before, and the years. Surely somewhere there was a man who would fill the ache in her heart.

Lily closed her eyes and whispered to the ceiling, "Hold him close, Annie. He is a man worthy of all your love."

Finally, deep sobs racked her body. Lily stifled them and buried her face in the pillow.

Later Jesse held open the front door of the old farmhouse, and Annie slipped inside. He followed her, and the stairs creaked on their climb upward.

Annie whispered to him in the darkness. "Your grandparents are going to hear us for sure, with two people on the stairs."

He chuckled softly. "I'll explain in the morning. Moonlight strolls are reasonable with the stress we—or rather you—are under."

"Thanks for finding me outside." Annie paused at the top of the stairs and reached for his hand. "It meant so much to me."

"I'm glad I heard you go down." He squeezed her hand. "No more nightmares, now."

Her laugh was soft. "I doubt if there is much time left for sleep, let alone nightmares."

"I think that was the dawn stirring the horizon," he agreed.

"Goot night then," Annie whispered, and moments later her bedroom door creaked.

Jesse found his way down the hall to his own door and stepped inside. The moonlight was still bright in the window, and he walked over to push back the drapes. The split-rail fence ran along this side of the house, where he had stood beside Annie. She had seemed so comfortable with him, so close to his heart, and yet they were not on the same page. Annie was in the middle of a search for her English Mamm—and now a twin sister—while he was on his way home. He had seen enough of the world out there and longed for peace and community. Those had always been part of Annie's life, but would she leave the community behind when she found her birth family?

The bonding they had felt tonight in the bright moonlight was not enough to build a life together. In his head he knew that, but his heart said otherwise. He had come close to kissing her while his arms were wrapped around her. The woman had stirred the depths of his emotion. Would Annie have spurned his kisses? Her heart had been open, but he had refrained. He couldn't take advantage of Annie's pain. He didn't want that injury between them, a doubt that would linger long after the sweetness of her lips had faded. He had better wait. Fate held so much in its hands, circumstances in the days ahead that they could not control.

Jesse sat on the bed to pull on his socks. He would not be able to sleep again tonight. Not with the memory of Annie's moonlit face fresh in his mind, or the strength of her fingers wrapped in his. He might as well head down to the kitchen and put on the coffeepot. His grandmother wouldn't mind. She might even understand if he explained his dilemma, but he wouldn't do that either. Silence was better. The pain in his heart should be borne alone. Tonight, he had the memory of Annie's closeness, and that was enough.

9

After breakfast that morning, Jesse's Malibu drove slowly down the side roads of Lancaster County and turned into a long gravel driveway. A small white bungalow—the *Dawdy Haus*, which was the grandparents' home—sat behind the sprawling two-story farmhouse with its wraparound porch. The red barn with wooden fences and pasture gates completed the picture of a prosperous Lancaster County farm.

Riding in the back seat, Annie leaned forward for a better view. "Should we go to the main house first, or right to the Dawdy Haus?"

"We'd best make our introductions at the house," Jesse suggested.

He came to a stop beside a buggy parked near the huge barn doors, and the three of them clambered out of the car. When no one appeared, Jesse led the way up to the farmhouse. Annie hung back while Lily knocked on the front door.

A young woman opened with a pleasant smile on her face. "Goot morning. What can I do for you?"

"We're Lily and Annie Miller, and this Jesse Yoder." Lily motioned with her hand. "We're staying at Jesse's grandparents' place."

The woman nodded. "Yah, I know them."

Lily hurried on. "They sent us over to speak with Mose and Susie Wagler. We think they used to volunteer their time at the Hope Clinic in Lancaster."

The woman's smile didn't dim. "I don't know about volunteering their time at the Hope Clinic, but Mose and Susie are my grandparents.

They should be up by now, if you wish to walk on over and knock on the Dawdy Haus door."

"Thank you," Lily told her, and they followed her point.

The young woman stayed in the doorway and waved to them as they turned the corner of the house.

"If Mose and Susie are that friendly," Annie said, "maybe there is hope that we will finally find answers."

"All Lancaster County Amish are friendly," Jesse assured her.

Annie held her breath when Lily stepped forward again and approached the door of the small bungalow. An elderly woman, bent over with age and leaning on a cane, answered Lily's knock.

"Goot morning," the woman said brightly.

"We were just over to the main farmhouse—" Lily began.

"Yah, I saw from the kitchen window. I'm Susie. I don't know you, so you must be visitors to the area."

Lily forced a smile. "I'm Lily Miller. This is my sister Annie and he is Jesse Yoder. His grandparents are local, but we're from Nebraska."

"Well, this is a treat!" Susie proclaimed. "Won't you come in? Mose is resting on his rocker. We've already had breakfast or I'd invite you to eat with us."

"Oh, we didn't come for breakfast," Lily assured her. "Jesse's grandmother feeds us quite well."

"I don't doubt it." Susie chuckled and stepped back from the doorway. "Come in and have a seat, and we'll see what we can do for you."

She led them into the living room and introduced them to her husband. "I'm delighted to meet you," the old man said. "What brings you all the way from Nebraska?"

"That's a long story," Lily said while they seated themselves on the couch.

Mose stroked his long white beard and contemplated Jesse. "I think I heard someone say you have family locally. Who are your grandparents?"

"Joseph and Lavina Yoder from over near Gap."

"Yah!" A big smile spread over Mose's face. "I know them well. They are goot people. But all of the Yoders are, I guess."

"Of course they are," Susie affirmed.

"So you are Annie and Lily Miller." Mose's attention shifted to the girls. "What's your long story?"

Annie forced the words out. "I am adopted, and we are looking for information on my history. We think you might be the couple who brought me and my twin sister to the midwife Olivia Raber, from Hope Clinic in Lancaster."

Mose stroked his beard for a long time. "Yah, that was us. I figured that one of the twins went to Enos and Lilliana Miller. I mean, Olivia Raber didn't tell us, but we could assume by which families adopted children soon afterward. But one doesn't just want to—"

"There is no shame in adoption, Mose!" Susie exclaimed. "You have said so yourself a thousand times."

"There is not," Mose agreed. "What I was trying to say is that the subject is a sensitive one, and emotions can be easily stirred. Are you not doing well with your adopted family, Annie?"

"Oh, that's not the trouble at all. There is nothing wrong there. Mamm and Daett could not have been better or kinder. They told me about my background when I was still young, and they promised that when I turned twenty-one they would tell me what they knew about my past. That wasn't much, but enough for me to trace the story this far. Could you tell us more? Perhaps who my Mamm and my sister are. I didn't know that I was a twin."

Mose nodded slowly. "Yah, you were twins. I told them that twins shouldn't be split up, but that was how things were worked out, I guess. I'm sure it would not be easy to take on two babies at once. And the government always thinks they know best, even when they don't. But here I go, speaking out of turn. We are just thankful that homes could be found for you amongst our people, as that was your Mamm's request."

"So you met her?" Annie leaned forward on the couch.

"I did," Mose admitted. "But Susie dealt with her most of the time. She had best tell you that part of the story."

Annie clasped and unclasped her hands while they waited.

"She was a pretty girl," Susie began. "She looked a little like you, Annie. Very sorrowful at the time, which was understandable, and struggling with what should be done. Her boyfriend had left her when he learned she was with child, and the poor woman was alone. She was but a child herself. Her parents wouldn't give her any support either. Everyone just wanted the problem to go away. How she had the courage to visit our clinic, I don't know. It's so much easier to end up at the other end of town, at that awful place where pregnancies are terminated." Susie paused to compose herself.

"So you spoke at length with my Mamm?" Annie's fingers dug into her palms until they hurt.

"Yah, I talked with her for a long time, and Mose prayed with us both. We didn't know if she would come back again, but she did the next week, with her wishes written out on paper, which we followed once the children were born."

"What was her name?" The question came from Lily.

Susie glanced at Mose. "Can we tell?"

"I think we must," he said. "Annie should know if she wishes to."

"Of course I do!" Annie nearly choked on the words.

Lily scooted closer and slipped her arm around Annie's shoulders.

"These are emotional issues," Mose said. "But the Lord can see us through them, and even make goot things come out of bad."

"Thank you," Annie whispered. "That encourages my heart."

A smile filled Susie's face. "Your Mamm's name was Alisha Mandarin. She was a sweet girl. I will never forget her sacrifice, and her tender heart toward her children."

"She was a goot woman," Mose agreed. "Alisha made the right choice."

"Do you know where my Mamm lives now?"

Susie glanced at Mose. "We do not. We did not keep track of her. Some things are best left in the Lord's hands."

"What about my sister, my twin? Does she live in the community?"

Susie didn't answer at first. Finally she said, "I'm sorry, Annie. We cannot tell you anything more. We may have already said too much."

Mose nodded on his rocker. "As I said, these are emotional subjects, and close to the heart. Only the Lord can touch there and not do more damage than goot."

"But please," Annie begged. "I have waited so long, and I am a twin. Can I not know?"

Mose's hand was on his beard again. "My heart is with you, Annie, and I would want nothing more than to tell you, but it is best if the word does not come from us. I will pray though, that the Lord reveal these secrets to you, in His time and in His way."

"Amen," Susie said. "We have been touched deeply by our work at the clinic, and our hearts were often torn, as they are even now."

"Thank you," Annie managed. "But I had to ask."

"We understand." Mose gave Annie a kind smile. "Someday we will live in a perfect world created by the Lord's own hand, where there is no suffering and no tears. My heart longs for that time."

Jesse rose to his feet and extended his hand. "Thank you, Mose, Susie. You have been kind to Annie this morning. May the Lord grant you kindness in return."

"We cling to that hope." Mose shook Jesse's hand. "And may the Lord go with you on your search."

Annie forced herself to stand, with Lily by her side. "Thank you so much again. You have been wunderbah to tell me this much."

As they left the old couple in their rocking chairs, Annie gave thanks for the kind hearts that had moved her a step farther in her journey. But where was she to go from here?

That evening, Grandma Yoder had the table laden with fried chicken, mashed potatoes, gravy, and boiled corn. Two pecan pies rested on the counter, cooling from their time in the oven. Lily hurried about the kitchen, setting the table and scolding at the same time. "You shouldn't have gone to all this trouble, Grandma. Not at your age."

Grandma Yoder snorted. "I feel spry as a spring chicken with all you youngsters in my house."

Even Annie smiled. She had been downcast on the drive back to Jesse's grandparents' farm, and through the subsequent spilling of their day's troubles. Grandma Yoder hadn't seemed surprised at the news. She must have anticipated trouble, given the generous spread on the table.

"This is exactly what we need," Lily added. "Thank you."

Obviously it would take more than a well-laden supper table to heal the hurt in Annie's heart. But a good supper was the right start after the closed door they had encountered. Something would come up. It had to.

"Supper!" Grandma called into the living room.

Grandpa and Jesse walked in, still engaged in hushed conversation. Everyone seated themselves at the table and bowed their heads for a prayer of thanks.

"What were you two talking about?" Grandma asked as they dug into the food.

Grandpa dished out a generous helping of mashed potatoes before he answered. "Just musing on where this search should go next."

"You have thought of something then?" Annie's voice was barely above a whisper.

"These roads are always full of twists and turns." Grandpa gave her a kind smile. "I know that may not comfort you much at the moment, but yah, Jesse and I have come up with a thought at least. It's worth checking out. I almost think I should go along, but then, maybe that would only make things worse."

"What is this you are thinking?" Grandma passed the plate of fried chicken to Lily. "Surely you don't plan to make a personal trip to see Mose and Susie? You know that Mose won't tell you anything more than he has told Annie."

Grandpa shook his head. "This is the question: How many adopted community children do we know from that time period?"

Grandma thought for a moment. "Not many, I suppose. But how does that help?"

"What is the one you do know of?" Grandpa took two pieces of chicken and passed the plate on.

"Mary Mast, Bishop Mast's child." Grandma didn't hesitate. "That's about it."

"Do you think Mary could be Annie's twin sister?"

"Does Mary look like Annie?" Lily asked before Grandma could answer.

Grandpa glanced at Annie. "I'd best not answer that question. False hope would not be goot at this point."

"Then she does!" Lily exclaimed.

"Now that I think about it, she does," Grandma agreed. "But it is best if we don't assume anything. Bishop Mast should answer the question himself."

"Then we'll be able to talk with him?"

Grandpa and Grandma were looking at each other.

"What is wrong?" Lily asked.

Grandpa grimaced. "Bishop Mast is a goot man, but he is the strictest of our bishops. Not even in southern Lancaster County is there a bishop who sticks closer to the *Ordnung*."

Jesse groaned. "I have heard of this bishop from my parents—in whispers."

"Let us not speak ill of Bishop Mast," Grandma chided. "He is the Lord's chosen leader among his people."

"Amen." Grandpa took some more chicken. "We must pray the Lord will soften Bishop Mast's heart."

Lily concentrated on her chicken. The food was delicious, but her appetite waned. Why was this search so difficult for Annie? Had not her sister suffered enough? Lily squeezed Annie's hand and whispered, "Please eat. You will need your strength tomorrow."

Annie nodded and tried to smile, but her effort was feeble.

An hour later Jesse sat outside on the front swing. The last of the sun's rays were on the horizon, a golden hue that would vanish in a moment. Annie and Lily were in the kitchen, washing the last of the supper dishes with Grandma. He should offer to help, but with three women the place was crowded.

"Come out and sit on the front porch with me when you're done," he had told Lily and Annie before he left the house.

They would be here any moment. Annie would still have tearstains on her face from the difficult day. They had made some progress, but the way ahead was anything but clear—and then there was Bishop Mast. He had faint memories from his youth, both of the man's fierce face while he preached and of his parents' whispered opinions of the man.

"He wouldn't have to offend so many people."

"There are better ways of enforcing the Ordnung without driving people off."

"The man is loyal to the church and dedicated to the Lord, but such zeal for the Ordnung!"

Somehow they would have to get past the man's defenses. Bishop Mast held to the old-fashioned ways in which some things were not talked about. Adoption would be among the subjects on that list.

Jesse sighed. He had enlisted for this journey because of his knowledge of English ways, but no one had expected an Amish bishop to stand in their path. Those were things he knew little about. If his grandfather was hesitant to intervene, he could about imagine how the next day would go.

Jesse pasted on a smile when the front door opened and Lily stepped out with Annie close behind her. "Done with the dishes?" he teased.

"Just like a man, relaxing on the front porch while the women work," Lily returned.

Jesse joined her laughter. Lily was fun to be around, but Annie was the one he wanted by his side at the moment and for reasons beyond comforting her. His heart melted with compassion—and with other feelings long dormant.

"You want to . . . ?" Jesse motioned with his hand for Annie to sit in the empty space beside him.

Annie accepted without protest. Lily settled in a chair a few feet away.

"Are you okay?" He reached for Annie's hand.

"I think so." Her voice was weak and strained. "Will this Bishop Mast tell us what we need to know?"

"We will pray that he does, and we will persuade him if he doesn't!" Lily said with great vehemence.

Jesse nodded. With Annie's nearness the words stuck in his mouth. She turned his tongue dry and his throat scratchy. Croaking an answer would only reveal the emotions he could not speak of.

"We will keep going," Lily continued. "This peaceful evening is a time to quiet our souls and repair our exhausted resources."

Jesse smiled and squeezed Annie's hand. She lifted her head to meet his gaze, and weakness stole through his entire body.

10

The kerosene lamp burned brightly on the dresser later that evening. The flames cast flickering shadows on the bedroom wall. Annie sat on the bed in her white nightgown, with her long hair flowing over her shoulders. The ends grazed the quilt. In front of her, Lily fastened the last string of her nightgown and preened in front of the dresser mirror.

"Jesse is not going to see you again tonight," Annie teased.

Lily gave her a baleful glance. "You sure have cheered up since an hour ago."

Annie sighed and ran her fingers through her hair. "I guess Jesse does that to me. He is such a blessing, and I have you to thank for suggesting that he bring us."

"I think Jesse is taking more than a brotherly interest in you." Lily swept her thick black hair over her shoulders and leaped into bed.

"Lily, don't say that." Annie drew her legs up onto the quilt and hugged her knees. "Jesse has been very kind to me, and I wouldn't want to spoil that by assigning motives to his attentions that aren't there."

"You know you like them, Annie." Lily studied her sister's face. "Admit the truth. The two of you are falling in love."

Annie laughed. "I don't think so. I mean, it wouldn't be right if I was. I have no right to Jesse's affections. He was your man from the beginning, and he still is."

"Jesse never returned my feelings, so he was never 'my man,'" Lily said. "I mean, he teases me, and we can share a goot laugh, but there is nothing more."

"You must not let your heart despair. This trip will be over soon, and once Jesse gets ready to settle down in the community, you are the right Frau for him. Don't tell me that isn't what you want anymore."

Lily stared at the ceiling. "I want to think that. I've always thought so, even after Jesse left the community for his long Rumspringa. Why else would I have avoided the other offers I have received? Now I'm not so sure. Seeing the two of you together, how Jesse comforts you, I begin to believe that you might be the Frau his heart desires."

"That's terrible." Annie hid her face in her hands. "You make me sound like a wild woman who runs the earth capturing the hearts of men who don't belong to her."

Lily winced. "I'm sorry. I didn't mean that. I know that your search for your Mamm is right."

"But it still looks like I'm out of my place," Annie insisted. "Jesse deserves better than me, much better. What if he becomes a bishop someday? My past would tarnish him. You know the community will never forget that I felt a need to leave and find my English Mamm. Even if I don't find her, I will have done what I have done."

"I wonder what Jesse's English girlfriend was like?" Lily mused.

"Lily!" Annie gasped.

"You know he had one in his Rumspringa!"

"We do not! How awful!"

"Not really. Jesse is a handsome man, and quite the charmer. If I were an English girl, I wouldn't hesitate to date him."

"Of course you wouldn't." Annie propped herself up on her elbow. "You like him."

"And you don't?"

Annie's face flushed.

"See? I know you do."

"Yah, but that doesn't mean what you imply." Annie's voice caught.

"I admit I have freely accepted Jesse's sympathy and comfort, but those have been for a reason other than romance. When my search is over, Jesse and I both know that things can't go any further."

"I think his girlfriend was pretty like you, and wild at heart." Lily peered across the room at Annie. "She certainly wasn't like me, a common homebody who keeps the garden."

Annie snorted. "You are pretty, Lily. You know that. Don't run yourself down."

Lily ignored the rebuke. "I think Jesse was very much in love with this English girl. I wonder what happened with her. Did they part in great sorrow, clinging to each other as they faced the inevitability of Jesse's return to the community?"

Annie laughed. "You are a dreamer. That's impossible."

"With Jesse, nothing is impossible."

"See, you are dreaming."

A smile crept across Lily's face. "Jesse makes me dream. I admit that, but can't you just see them, leaning against Jesse's Malibu and saying goodbye? Maybe she rode in the very seat I sat in this evening, holding Jesse's hand, gazing into his eyes in those last hours. Jesse would have told her the news gently, how it was time for him to return home, that he loved her so much, but he couldn't live life out there without the arms of the community to give him protection. Jesse would have asked her to return with him. In great agony she would have turned him down. Neither of them was able to deny the truth in their hearts, and so they were torn asunder. I wonder how they parted? Maybe with a kiss? One last, long, lingering, passionate kiss—for old times' sake, for what could never be? For what they both wanted so much—just to be together in a perfect world where hard choices would face no one, choices for which neither of them was to blame?"

"Like finding my Mamm," Annie mused. "You are only making my point. I am not the Frau Jesse needs, and I'm sorry if I have taken liberties that weren't mine to take. I hope you won't hold them against me. I don't intend to steal your boyfriend."

"He's not my boyfriend." Lily forced a smile. "You're not stealing anything."

"You are very understanding." Annie settled back on the pillows. "Goot night."

Sweet sleep swept over her. Worry would not solve the problems that lay ahead of them. Annie took a deep breath and willed her mind to cease its whirl. Jesse's handsome face rose in front of her, but she was too tired to object. He was such a comfort and a joy. He would make Lily a very goot husband someday.

Lily watched out of the corner of her eye as Annie drifted off to sleep. She should join her sister in slumber, but tears threatened now that she was alone. Her words had been brave, and she had tried to say the right thing, but her heart throbbed with pain. For so many years she had longed for Jesse's attentions and waited for his return. To see Jesse give Annie freely what he had never given her cut deeply. Her reasoning did little to ease the pain. One could not demand a man return her affections, and no one needed a clingy Frau. Maybe that's what she had always been, hanging on to a dream that could never come true. Maybe this was the best medicine for her, seeing with her own eyes how Jesse was when he opened his heart. The pain stung deeply, but there might also be healing ahead.

"Let it come quickly," Lily whispered to the ceiling.

She turned her head to glance at Annie. Her sister's breathing had slowed, and a look of peace crept over Annie's face. Lily didn't usually talk to herself. This was a new road she was on. She had never faced the reality that Jesse might return from his Rumspringa and settle down with another Frau. She should have, but she hadn't. How foolish she had been. It shouldn't have taken seeing Annie with Jesse for the truth to sink in. Jesse had not returned her affections in the past for a reason. The man wanted something else in his Frau. If he did settle for her, that's what it would be—settling. Jesse was worthy of more than that. She could not live with herself if she knew Jesse would always be aware he could have done better.

Lily blinked back the tears and slipped out from under the quilt. She walked over to the bedroom window to gaze into the night. The moon hadn't risen yet, and only the dim outline of the split-rail fence was visible in the heavy dusk. She should go outside and roam the night as Annie had done the other morning. Jesse wouldn't follow her though. She was sure of that, and the moon wouldn't be up for a while yet. Stumbling around in the darkness would only get her stubbed toes, and no relief from the pain in her heart.

Sleep was the answer. That was better than tiptoeing around the house and causing a stir. Lily wiped her eyes with the corner of her nightgown and crossed the room to climb back under the covers.

Down the hall, Jesse had been asleep for over an hour, with the memory of Annie's hand in his as he drifted away. But her tender smile faded in his dreams, replaced quickly by that of another girl, who laughed beside him in his car, leaning across the console to hug him and kiss his cheek.

Jesse muttered under his breath, unable to turn back the dream. He wanted to shout a warning to himself, this man in the car with the beautiful girl, as they careened down the highway and collided with a large animal on the road. He should have been paying attention, but she had been holding tight to his arm, her gaze fixed on his face. He did not blame her. He blamed himself for focusing on her loveliness instead of the road. She screamed at the impact. Yolanda always screamed in his dreams as the tire blew and they went over the embankment.

Jesse awoke, crying out in the darkness, his body soaked in sweat. He sat upright in bed and listened. What if someone had heard him? This had to stop, his awakenings from terror and yelling into the night. He no longer lived alone in an apartment. Jesse wiped his face with his hand and listened. All was silent in the hall outside, but he had to know if the girls had heard. They wouldn't come to his bedroom to inquire before morning, but there would be a light on in their room, whispers perhaps as Annie and Lily debated whether a burglar had invaded the house. Grandma and Grandpa wouldn't have awakened. They slept deeply.

Jesse threw the covers off and pulled on his clothes in the darkness. Barefoot, he tiptoed into the hallway. There was only silence beyond the bedroom door where Annie and Lily slept. He listened for a moment. Perhaps he hadn't been as loud as he thought he had. Jesse continued down the stairs, the groan of wood harsh in the stillness of the night. This was how he had heard Annie leave the other night, but no one stirred in the bedroom behind him. What if Lily heard and came out? He could tell her he had had nightmares and he was out for a breath of fresh air. Lily would believe him, but she wouldn't join him.

They were like that—their relationship kept on the edges. Lily wanted his affections, but she had never asked. Not like other girls had asked. Not like Yolanda. Yet he would have said no to Lily all those years ago, which meant that he was to blame. He had intended to return home and rectify that problem, but he had not planned on Annie. Even before Lily had come to him wanting help with the search for Annie's Mamm, he knew he couldn't open his heart to her.

Jesse opened the front door of the farmhouse and crept into the night. The grass was cold beneath his feet, the bright moonlight missing. He wanted Annie with him, and yet he didn't. That was his problem. He wanted and he didn't want at the same time. The car crash that night, with its metal wrapped around the tree, had forever doomed him. He had been thwarted in his intentions twice. Once in his Rumspringa when he had planned to join Yolanda's world. Now, back in the community when he planned to make peace with Lily. Both decisions had failed. Was he doomed to a life of failure?

He had lost his heart when Yolanda had lost her life, and he appeared ready to break Lily's in two. What was wrong with him? Yolanda's loss was senseless, without meaning, a tragedy that rightly provoked nightmares. He should suffer for the rest of his life for his carelessness, his recklessness that night in the car.

He had been thrown from car upon impact because he wasn't wearing a seat belt. Yolanda had also been without one, but the tree had been on her side. That was why he had been spared. Yolanda deserved to live, not him.

Jesse found the wooden rail of the fence with his hands just as he stubbed his toe against the post. The pain tingled up his leg, and he grimaced. He should slam his foot against the wood, but nothing would bring Yolanda back.

What would Annie say when she learned the truth of his past? He knew how Lily would respond—with acceptance. Lily had the ways of the community deep in her heart. That's why he had gone back to where things would be safe and secure. Yolanda had been safe and secure, but in a different way. It was the difference between a rock fixed on land and a ship on the high seas. Lily was the rock and Annie was the ship. Already he had climbed on board and tasted the salt of the sea with Yolanda. Annie was leaving for ports unknown, and he couldn't resist the temptation to follow her. How wrong this was of him. He must stop—but he couldn't. He deserved the nightmares and much worse punishment. Maybe he didn't deserve Annie. Maybe he was afraid of winning her—and then losing her as he had lost Yolanda.

Annie thought he was a man who could comfort her, support her, and perhaps find the answers she needed. *If Annie only knew!* Jesse groaned and let go of the split-rail fence. The splinters had penetrated the skin, but he didn't care. Perhaps the pain would keep the nightmares away.

Jesse stubbed his toe again on the porch as he went back inside, but he didn't stop until he was in the bedroom and under the covers.

11

Annie clung to Grandma Yoder on the front porch of the old farmhouse soon after dawn the next morning, drawing strength from her comforting presence.

"The Lord go with you." Grandma patted Annie on the back.

"Should we maybe wait until later in the day? The bishop might be in a better mood?"

Grandma shook her head. "Early in the morning is the best time for us old people." A smile flitted across her face.

"Speak for yourself," Grandpa added in the background, and everyone laughed in spite of the circumstances.

"Thanks so much to both of you for everything." Annie gave Grandma another long hug.

When Annie let go, Grandpa stuck out his hand. "The best to you today. We'll be waiting for goot news when you come back."

"I hope so," Annie choked out. "You have been very kind and helpful."

"The pleasure is all ours," Grandma assured her.

Jesse took Annie by the elbow and escorted her down the porch steps with Lily beside them. Grandpa and Grandma Yoder were still waving when they pulled out of the driveway.

"They are such sweet people." Annie wiped away a tear. "You are so blessed, Jesse."

His smile was kind. "You have parents who love you too."

"I know." The tears stung again. "And yet I am not satisfied. It's shameful."

"Don't scold yourself," Lily spoke up. "Let's just hope dear Bishop Mast has had his morning coffee."

Annie stifled a gasp as Jesse chuckled. "That's not respectful."

"I know," Lily agreed, but she didn't appear repentant in the least. "I can't shake my premonition that this day will not turn out well. I slept fitfully because of it."

Jesse grimaced. "I didn't have a peaceful night either."

"Are you both worrying about me?" Annie leaned forward. "This is awful. I'm so sorry. I really am."

Jesse forced a laugh. "I don't think you are to blame for my night's disturbance. So don't feel bad."

Lily gave Annie a weak smile. "I'm sorry for my outburst. Here you are at the center of this whirlwind, and I'm the one complaining."

Annie didn't respond. What was there to say? Besides, Jesse was slowing his car for the driveway ahead of them.

"Looks like we're here," Jesse confirmed. "Last chance for prayers."

No one laughed as they pulled in the long lane that led to a staid, two-story white farmhouse on a hilltop with a sprawling barn on the slope.

Jesse parked his car near the front walks. "Is this the best port of entry?"

"I'd try the barn," Lily suggested. "Face the lion in his den."

"You are funny this morning," Jesse told her. "I think I'll go for Grandma first."

"I don't think the bishop's wife is a grandma yet," Lily said. "No one said anything about Mary being wed, and she is an only child."

"Just because no one has said she is married does not mean she isn't," Jesse argued.

Annie groaned. "Please stop bickering, you two. There is enough hardship in this day."

Jesse laughed. "Maybe you are right. Let's face the lion in his den. Bishop might take offense if he thought we made inroads into his family before we consulted him."

Jesse drove forward and came to a stop beside the barn door. The three travelers climbed out and looked around. There was no sign of anyone around, not even a shadow shifting in the window of the tall while farmhouse.

"Visitors not welcome," Lily murmured to no one in particular.

"Maybe we should have come in a buggy," Jesse quipped.

"We're Amish and we look Amish!" Lily declared. She appeared ready to lead an assault on the barn door.

Annie clutched Lily's hand a second before the hinges squeaked and a bearded form appeared with a black wool hat pulled over his ears.

"The bishop," Jesse whispered.

Fortunately, Bishop Mast appeared not to have heard the remark. He was studying them with an intense gaze, but he hadn't moved from the barn door.

Annie forced her feet to move, and the others followed. "Goot morning." Her voice barely worked. "Are you Bishop Mast?"

"Yah!" His gaze didn't shift. "And you are?"

"Annie Miller, and this is my sister, Lily, and our friend Jesse Yoder. We're from southern Nebraska."

His gaze shifted between them. "I see. I have heard of the place. How many districts do you have?"

"Two, I think," Annie told him.

"You don't know?" His words were sharp.

"No, I do," Annie stammered. "We just divided up two years ago, and there is talk of a third district."

"You are growing then?" The bishop's hand moved on the barn latch, but he didn't close the door. Apparently they were worth a continued conversation. His gaze shifted again. "That is goot to hear, even for a liberal Amish congregation."

Annie ignored the insult. "We were wondering if you could help us—"

His uplifted hand stopped her. "First things first. Tell me what three young people are doing in Lancaster County, one of them not related to the other two?" His sharp glance took in Jesse. "And to top things off, driving around the country in an English automobile. Are any of you baptized?" His beard jerked downward to indicate the long Amish dresses. "You look decent enough, and yet—"

"Lily and I are baptized," Annie said.

That left Jesse, but she didn't know how to explain the complicated situation.

"He's not wed to one of you, then?"

Annie caught her breath. "No!"

"That is goot."

Lily's words cut the air. "These are indecent questions, Bishop. Annie and I have a reputation of the highest moral standing in our community, without a stain on our character. Neither of us would wed a man who had not joined the community. I don't know why you insist on insulting us. You don't even know us."

The bishop appeared unperturbed by the outburst. "Seeing a person is knowing a person, young lady, but I will excuse your ignorance and forward manner. You are from a liberal community and obviously not taught well."

Jesse cleared his throat. "Good bishop, there is no reason to quarrel. I am not yet baptized because I have just returned from my Rumspringa, but am ready to settle down with a proper Frau and take up my duties in the community. In the meantime, Annie has always wanted to find her birth Mamm, and I agreed to take her on the search before I got rid of my automobile. I intend to sell it just as soon as we find the answers her heart requires."

The bishop turned his piercing gaze on Jesse. "That sounds like a bunch of excuses, young man, but I will leave that judgment to the bishop of your own community—liberal though it is. I hope the bishop has some sense."

"I don't know why you keep saying that," Lily shot back. "Our community is just as Amish as the Lancaster Amish are."

The bishop grunted. "We will leave that point in the Lord's hands. So this Annie is adopted. Are her parents not kind to her? Has there been trouble at home?"

"My parents are wonderful," Annie answered. "They have always been open to me about my adoption, but they also understood my desire to someday meet my real Mamm. They told me that I could search for her after my twenty-first birthday."

"Why are you not wed?" the bishop asked. "You are a goot-looking girl." He glanced at Jesse. "There is no reason some man would not want your hand in marriage."

Lily didn't hide her outrage. "Is that all you have to say after Jesse told you why we are here? Annie's heart needs closure in this matter. Finding her birth mother is only responding to a call the Lord has placed in every child's heart for their Mamm."

The bishop moved closer. "I will not have you lecturing me, young woman. These are liberal things you are telling me, speaking of the Lord's things as if you were ordained. I thought to hold my tongue about your so-called 'Amish' community, but I see that the whispers I heard about the place have been correct. Let me tell you this. You will not bring these wild ideas into our community. So whatever counsel you thought to ask of me, I will not provide. Now will you please leave?"

"We didn't come to ask counsel," Jesse said. "You have an adopted daughter yourself. We came to—"

"What I have and don't have is none of your concern," the bishop cut in. "Mary is not like Annie here, wandering the earth in search of who knows what. Mary has settled her heart with thankfulness for what the Lord gave her while she was a child—a goot and godly home. Mary has no complaints and is happy in my house. Now go!"

Annie forced the words out. "Mary had a sister, a twin sister, did she not? A girl who was adopted by my parents."

The bishop's face turned red. "I don't know what you are talking about, young woman. Mary is our daughter, and soon to be wed to an upright man, as you should be yourself. That Mary is adopted is in the past, and I will not discuss the matter. Mary is no longer an English woman, and certainly does not have an English sister."

"I am not an English woman," Annie protested. "I am Amish."

"You are acting like one," the bishop said. "It is the same thing."

He whirled about and pulled the barn door shut behind him.

"I guess that's that." Jesse wiped his brow.

"Did I ever say too much, and to a bishop!" Lily appeared subdued for a second. "I'll have to catch my breath and learn how to control myself."

Annie blinked back the tears. "You said nothing wrong, Lily. I am the one who should have been more careful with my words, or used other ones. I don't know."

"Let's get out of here," Lily said. "I still feel guilty, but that was also awful behavior from an Amish bishop, slamming the barn door in our faces."

They silently climbed back into the Malibu and Jesse drove out of the lane as a small cloud of dust rose behind them.

"The nerve of the man!" Lily declared a mile down the road.

She took several deep breaths to calm herself. Annie was crying in the back seat from the sound of the stifled sobs. Lily knew her sister did not deserve the treatment the bishop had dished out.

"So I guess our premonitions were correct," Jesse said with a meaningful glance at Lily.

"I'm telling every little detail to your grandparents," Lily declared. "Perhaps something can be done."

"Like what?" Jesse lifted his eyebrows.

"Something! Anything!" Lily waved her hand in the air. "The insults the man gave us, and the lectures. Surely not every bishop is like him. The others might speak up, and maybe rebuke him. This can't go on."

Jesse grimaced. "He's the bishop of his district and we were on his home ground. My grandparents warned us."

"So you're saying nothing can be done? I mean, we're Amish like he is, regardless of what the man says. I'll call home to the phone shack and see if Daett can do anything about this. A phone call back from our bishop might help."

"Please don't," Annie begged from the back seat. "You know the community never approved of my search, and if they hear of the trouble we have stirred up in Lancaster . . . why, we should be thankful that Bishop Mast doesn't call Deacon Bontrager with the tale of what happened today."

"I think Annie's right," Jesse agreed. "Not that I am a church member, as the bishop reminded me, but that's my humble opinion."

"So you are just letting this go?" The anger was back in Lily's voice. "You know this is the end of the road. If we don't find proof that Mary is Annie's sister, along with the other details Bishop Mast is hiding—"

"Don't stir up more trouble," Annie pleaded. "I'm still shaking over what happened back there."

Lily reached for Annie's hand. "You did nothing wrong in searching for your Mamm. We're going to find her. I don't know how, but we've come this far, and we can't go back."

Annie whimpered and squeezed Lily's hand. "Thank you. I don't know what I have done to deserve such kindness from both of you—from everyone really."

"Except Bishop Mast!" Lily let go of Annie's hand and glared forward again. She had to calm herself. Grandpa Yoder's place was just ahead, and she couldn't arrive in the middle of a fit. Whatever Bishop Mast had done, an angry Amish woman would not make a goot impression on anyone.

"Are you okay?" Jesse asked.

Lily didn't answer.

Jesse brought the car to a stop, and he climbed out to wait while the girls walked around to stand beside him. He wanted to give Annie a hug, but this was too public a place for such blatant comfort. He nudged her lightly with his elbow instead. "I'm sorry about what happened. You didn't deserve that."

The front door of the house burst open, and his grandmother hurried toward them. "You're back already. With goot news, I hope?"

"I'm afraid not," Jesse told her.

His grandmother's face fell. "But surely—"

"Bishop Mast was awful!" Lily spat out the words.

Annie gasped and let go of Jesse's hand. "My sister didn't mean that the way it sounded. She—"

"I feel guilty, but I meant every word," Lily interrupted. "Bishop Mast was awful!"

"I am sure there was a reason for how Bishop Mast acted," Jesse said. "We have to step back and take a deep breath. That's my suggestion after the morning we had. You girls can help Grandma in the house today, and I'll work with Grandpa in the barn. After all, we have been staying here."

"Jesse, stop that," his grandmother ordered. "Tell me what happened."

The sad tale spilled out of the three young people. Grandpa appeared from the barn in the middle of the outburst and stood silently, listening.

"I had hoped for something better from Bishop Mast," Grandpa concluded at the end. "I am sorry the bishop behaved so badly."

"Like I said, the bishop likely had his reasons." Jesse shifted the toe of his shoe in the gravel driveway. "Maybe Mary's engagement isn't secured in spite of what Bishop Mast claimed, and then we show up with tales from the past. The man acted scared, if you ask me."

A glance passed between his grandparents. "Mary seems happy with Ben Wengerd," Grandma Yoder said.

"We must not imagine things about the bishop and his family," his grandfather concluded. "There are always reasons we cannot see."

Jesse nodded. "I was just trying to say that the man seemed sensitive about the subject—too sensitive. I suggest we wait a day or so and let this morning blow over. I can help around the place today, and we can plan an outing tomorrow. I'd love to show the girls Lancaster County."

"That's perfect!" his grandfather declared with a grin. "I have the manure spreader hooked up and ready to go. Thanks for volunteering, Jesse."

Jesse groaned while everyone else managed a laugh. "I'm going to change into old clothes," he told them. "I'll see you later."

He left the girls with Grandma's arms wrapped around them and Grandpa heading back toward the barn with a grin still on his face.

12

The following morning, Annie paused on the Yoders' front porch with the sun's rays blazing across the wooden floor. Only yesterday morning she had stood here with hope strong in her heart. Today those emotions had fled, perhaps never to return. Every road so far on her search had led to a dead end. Jesse's suggestion that they spend the day touring Lancaster County didn't really help. Sure, seeing the sights of the most famous Amish community in the world was okay, and spending time with Jesse was even better, but both of them knew where that would lead—nowhere.

Annie glanced over her shoulder when the front door opened. Lily stepped closer to whisper, "I'm not going with you and Jesse today."

"Lily." Annie pulled in her breath. "I was expecting—you must really come along."

Lily closed the door behind her. "I really don't want to, Annie. I'll spend the day here with Grandma Yoder. She could use my help with the garden."

"Then I should also stay!" Annie exclaimed. "I can work in the house, cleaning, sewing, baking pies for tonight's supper perhaps."

Lily shook her head. "Jesse wants to go, and you should go along."

"But—"

Lily held firm. "No protesting. Jesse wants to be with you. Let's be honest about that. Maybe this is for the best—you and him, getting ready for your new life together when we return to the community."

"Don't say that."

"It is for the best," Lily continued, undeterred. "You will need someone to comfort your heart if this search comes to nothing."

Lily stopped when Jesse appeared around the corner of the house. Lily gave him a quick smile and dashed back inside.

"What was that all about?" Jesse asked.

"Lily doesn't want to come today. Maybe we should call this off and head straight back to Nebraska. We've taken up enough of your time and your grandparents' hospitality, and there are two long days of travel ahead—"

Jesse stopped her with a touch on her arm. "I'm sorry that Lily isn't coming, but I still want to spend another day here. I haven't been back in years. And it will be much more enjoyable with you along."

"Really?" Annie met his gaze.

"Yah." His eyes twinkled. "If for no other reason than to see the looks of jealousy from the other men when they see you with me."

Annie suddenly forgot how to breathe. "You don't mean that."

"I do. Come." He took her hand. "This will be a great day." His hold on her hand tightened.

She avoided his gaze. Her feelings for Jesse were another dead end, but she couldn't resist. Maybe there would be sweet memories from today at least, as there were from the night Jesse had comforted her beside the split-rail fence. His arms had been so protective around her.

"All right," she murmured. She must not read too much into Jesse's request.

"I'm glad," he said. "Let me run back into the house and talk to Lily for a minute. I'll be right back."

Annie stepped off the porch and headed down the sidewalk. The barn door opened as she arrived at Jesse's Malibu.

"Are you about ready to leave?" Grandpa Yoder called out.

Annie forced a smile. "Jesse is in the house talking with Lily. She's staying here today and helping Grandma in the garden. I should stay too and help with the housework—"

"You should go." Grandpa interrupted her with a smile. "I hope you have a goot day with Jesse. Perhaps he can cheer you up, better than two old people anyway. Lavina can handle the cleaning." Grandpa finished with a chuckle.

"We should repay you somehow," Annie protested. "You have already done more than I ever could have expected. I can't thank you enough."

"So you think this is the end of the road?"

Annie hung her head. "I'm afraid so. I don't see what else we can do. From how things look we will be heading back to Nebraska tomorrow."

Grandpa wrinkled his face in sympathy. "May the Lord comfort you then. At times He's the only one who can in those dark moments when we can't understand what is happening."

Annie looked away. "I tried my best. Everyone did."

She could say what she wished, but her dream would never die. Not until she had seen her English Mamm's face. It was a desire the Lord had placed in her heart. *Why then is the Lord not helping us?*

"There's Jesse now," Grandpa said. "I'd best be getting busy." He gave Jesse a little wave before he ambled toward the barn.

"Ready?" Jesse asked as he approached.

"What did you need to talk to Lily about?" Annie looked up into his face.

He opened the car door for her. "I made sure Lily knew she was welcome to come along, but she doesn't want to."

Annie hesitated before she climbed in. This had always been Lily's seat. Tomorrow Lily would sit here again, but Annie couldn't ride all over Lancaster County seated in the back, like Jesse was a hired driver. A smile played on her face.

"What?" Jesse asked as he started the car.

"I was thinking how it would look if I rode in the back seat today."

He laughed. "That would be silly. I like you up here with me." He drove out of the driveway. "Where to first?" he asked, taking a right turn.

"I think you would know better than I do," she demurred. "Any place is fine with me."

"Sounds like you will make some man a submissive Amish Frau someday."

"Jesse," she scolded. "How awful."

"I think you will," he said, appearing quite unrepentant.

Annie kept silent, her gaze fixed out of the side window as Jesse wove into the busy morning traffic. They climbed north out of town, past rolling farms and open countryside. They passed a sign that read *Whitehorse.*

"I used to peer out of my parents' buggy at these fields," he said, "with my brothers and sisters crowded in the back seat with me. I didn't appreciate what I was seeing back then, the peacefulness of this county. I saw life as boring. Now I've come to value tradition and community."

"Your Rumspringa taught you that?"

"I guess." He shrugged. "Maybe I would have found my way back without it, but it seems unlikely."

"What were your nightmares about the other night?"

He glanced at her with wide eyes.

"You said you had some—bad ones apparently. Lily asked, but you didn't explain."

Jesse studied the road as they navigated another sharp curve. He motioned with his head. "Look at that view, with the manicured farms, and the horse teams working in the distance."

"You are avoiding the question."

"Maybe."

"I want to know," she insisted.

"I'm not sure you do. Sometimes it's like that. We think we want to know—"

"Like me wanting to find my Mamm?"

"I didn't mean that." He gave her a pained look.

"Tell me what your nightmares are about, Jesse. Please."

"I have different ones," he dodged again.

"This is a dream that comes back often, isn't it?" She took his hand.

"I killed my Rumspringa girlfriend, Annie." The words came out quickly, almost under his breath.

Her grip tightened. "I don't believe that."

He kept his eyes on the road. "I hit a large dog while I was driving too fast, and I couldn't recover. We blew a tire and went over an embankment. From there, we were thrown into a tree."

"Oh, Jesse." Her fingers dug deep into his arm.

"I know. I thought I had the world at my fingertips, then it was gone."

"What did they say about the accident?"

"You mean, what was I charged with?"

Annie nodded.

"Nothing. There was the dog and the blown tire. Neither of us was wearing our seat belts. Which saved me when I was thrown out of the car. The tree was on Yolanda's side."

"That's a sweet name."

"She was a sweet girl."

"Did you love her?"

Jesse didn't answer.

"Do you still love her?"

He gave a heavy sigh. "I'll never forget Yolanda, or my part in her death. I'm a scarred man, Annie. I may not look so on the outside, but inside I'm damaged goods."

"Is this why you came back from your Rumspringa?"

"Isn't any reason a goot reason?"

"I'm not trying to accuse you. I just want to know."

He nodded.

"There's nothing wrong with that."

He looked away. "You are understanding and kind, much like Yolanda."

"You don't think Lily would be?"

"Must we speak about Lily?" He slowed the car and pulled into a pasture lane. His smile was thin. "Do you want to get out here? There's a nice view."

Annie pulled her gaze away from his troubled eyes. Jesse climbed out and came around to open the car door. She slipped her hand into his and he didn't object.

His gaze was fixed on the rolling horizon. "Lancaster County doesn't get any better than right here. This is what the tourists come for, but they get sidetracked by the gift shops, quilts, and baked goods."

"The Lord can heal your heart, Jesse." She gazed into his face. "This is really why you wanted to stay another day in Lancaster County, isn't it?"

He pulled her close. "How is it that you always understand me?"

"Do you object?"

"No. Should I?"

"Yah!"

He smiled down at her. "I don't think so."

She studied his face. "We are two broken souls. You know that. We both speak of healing, but we are not healed. I have to find my Mamm, which might not happen now. I'll never forget her though. The pain will be like a spring in my heart, ready to burst for the slightest reason. That's not something an Amish man will want to deal with. And you—you will never forget a sweet girl like Yolanda."

"And yet we are here. Doesn't that mean anything?"

"You are asking me? I'm the woman who led you across the country on a wild goose chase."

"This has not been a wild goose chase. We are not at the end of the journey."

She shook her head. "We can never be together. Not in that way. You know this, and so do I."

He pulled her close, closer than he had that night beside the split-rail fence. Annie held her breath. She knew she should resist, but she didn't.

"Annie, look at me," he said softly.

When she did, the blaze of his eyes cut through her, and her knees trembled. She reached for him, and he pressed his lips against hers. Annie clung to him as his arms tightened.

"Jesse!" She tried to breathe.

"We shouldn't be doing this," he whispered.

"I know, but I don't care." She pulled his lips back to hers.

Lily peered out from behind a tree behind the Hope Clinic and waited. Her gaze was fixed on the back window, but no hand waved back, their agreed-upon signal that she should make her move. What a fix they would both be in if someone caught them, yet Wanda Coleman had agreed readily to the venture when Lily had made the call from the phone shack down the road from Jesse's grandparents' place.

"I need to call someone before I begin work on the garden," she had told Grandma Yoder. A harder sell had been required when Wanda drove in to pick her up after only an hour's work in the garden. "I'll be back before long."

From the look on Grandma Yoder's face, she had an idea of what was going on, but she was wise enough not to protest.

"It'll be a breeze, and we'll be right home again," Wanda had assured her on the drive into Lancaster. "It's not right that Annie doesn't know who her birth mother is. I'll tell them I need to look at some of my mother's papers, which is true, and I'll leave copies by the unlatched window. At the worst they will think someone left the window open. Even if they figure I was to blame, nothing will be missing."

But first Wanda would have to find the records. Already thirty minutes had ticked past without a hand in the windowpane, unless she had missed the signal. Lily stilled her rapid breathing and kept watch. Surely such a simple error wouldn't be their undoing. This was the Lord's inspiration and she would have to trust Him. Even with her bold ways, she would not have thought of asking Wanda to copy records from the Hope Clinic. She was an Amish girl, and she planned to settle down as a proper Amish Frau. This was not how such a person acted.

Lily froze when Wanda's hand waved in the window. She darted to the window and pressed against the pane. The wooden window groaned under the pressure of her hand but moved slowly upward. The papers lay just inside. Lily grabbed them and gently lowered the pane back into place. Every sound was magnified in her ears, but no one appeared in the room inside.

Lily ducked low and scurried south in the alley. "Go left, and down one block," Wanda had instructed. "I'll be waiting in a parking space across from the drugstore."

Lily folded and tucked the papers into her satchel before she burst out of the alley. Any second she would hear voices yelling, "Stop, thief!"

But she had stolen nothing. These were just copies and Annie's by right. What law could cut the heartstrings between Mamm and child?

Lily searched the street and found the sign for the drugstore ahead of her. Wanda pushed open the car door as she reached the vehicle.

Lily leaped inside. "Are they after us?"

Wanda giggled. "No, but I feel a little like we robbed a bank."

"Oh, don't say that," Lily moaned. "I already feel guilty."

"We did nothing wrong!" Wanda declared. "And look what I got for you."

Lily unfolded the papers. The name leaped out at her—Alisha Mandarin. The address was in Lancaster County.

"We did it," Wanda sang out as they raced out of town.

Lily stared at the papers. She had seen the address of Annie's Mamm before her sister, but Annie would understand. And there also was a twin baby listed, adopted by a Mr. and Mrs. Lester Mast. Tears filled Lily's eyes as she hugged the papers to her chest.

The late-afternoon sun hung on the horizon as Jesse drove back to his grandparents' place. They had spent the day driving around Lancaster County, stopping in at the usual tourist spots in spite of his words earlier in the day. He hadn't cared though. Everything had been a daze since his kiss with Annie on top of the hill above the town of Whitehorse. He had never planned to kiss another woman after Yolanda—at least not until he could offer her what he had not given Yolanda: home, safety, commitment, and his undying declaration of devotion.

Annie smiled sweetly. "I have so enjoyed our time together, Jesse."

"So have I, but I shouldn't have."

"Don't say it, Jesse. I know how things are between us, and how far apart we are. But thank you for this day. Lily doesn't have to know."

"You would keep secrets from your sister?"

The smile faded. "I don't seem to have much choice. And Lily will understand when it's time to tell her."

He nodded his acceptance of the arrangement.

"You have been kind to me. I'll never forget that, even when we head home tomorrow, and I'm in the back seat where I belong."

"But Annie—is there no hope for us?"

She stopped him with a touch on his arm. "We must accept what is and what can never be."

He slowed for his grandparents' driveway. There was no time for a protest. And what was there to say? He knew Annie spoke the truth.

"I'm still sorry."

"I know," she said. "So am I."

Jesse pulled to a stop by the barn, but before he could climb out, the front door of the house burst open and Lily raced across the lawn, waving papers at them.

13

Annie hung on to the armrest in the back seat of Jesse's Malibu as they bounced up Bishop Mast's driveway. *Slow down*, she wanted to tell Jesse, but maybe this was the best approach. It took great courage to face the wrath of the bishop, even with evidence. They could not back down though. With proof, they could get past Bishop Mast's stonewalling. Mary Mast was her twin sister, and they had the right to meet. More than that, they had the right to establish a relationship they had both been denied.

Had her parents known about her twin sister? Likely not. They would have told her if they had. That meant Bishop Mast had also been in the dark until they arrived yesterday with obviously upsetting news for him. No wonder the bishop had been disturbed.

"I see nothing of our dear bishop," Lily muttered from the front seat. She peered out as Jesse came to a stop by the front walks. "The house, Jesse?"

"This time, if you ask me, right straight to the house is the best approach."

Annie's fingers dug into the palms of her hands. What would they do without Jesse's common sense? Lily would charge straight to the barn and accost the bishop. That would get them nowhere. "I'm going in." Annie hopped out.

"I'm staying in the car," Lily told them. "My temper would get the best of me."

Jesse nodded and waited for Annie. He offered his elbow for

the trek up the sidewalk. She leaned against him. Did Jesse know that she felt likely to pass out before she arrived at the front door? She had held him close yesterday and kissed him. But things could not go any further. They both knew that.

"Thank you, Jesse." The words slipped out.

He smiled and patted her arm. "You'll get to meet your sister this morning."

Jesse always knew the right thing to say. Why couldn't she be the right Frau for him?

They climbed the porch steps and Jesse knocked on the door. She let go of his arm, but anyone watching through the window would have noticed their approach. They were not wed. Bishop Mast's family would know that information from their visit the other day. She should have stifled her desire for Jesse's comfort and presented a better image this morning. And what must Lily think of her public display of affection, despite her denials?

Annie blinked when the front door opened and a round-faced woman appeared. Clearly this was Bishop Mast's Frau, Rebecca.

"Yah?" Rebecca stood firmly in the half-open doorway.

"We are from Nebraska. We were—" Jesse began.

"I know who you are." The curt interruption came. "I thought my husband told you not to bother us again."

Jesse tried to smile. "You can't really expect that to happen, can you, Rebecca? We are Amish, after all. You have to see us somewhere. In church, if nothing else, so perhaps you want to see us here, now that we have proof. Mary is Annie's twin sister."

"You have proof of this?" Puzzlement played on Rebecca's face. "How?"

"I know you probably weren't told," Annie said. "And neither were my parents, who were always open and honest with me. I'm sure you have been the same way with Mary. But we have learned the truth. Mary and I are twins. We are family." Annie caught her breath and straightened. "It is right that we should meet each other and make up for the years we lost."

Rebecca's gaze swept up and down Annie's length. "I guess you are Amish. But wasn't there something about finding your birth Mamm? Mary is not about to join you on that journey."

"I wouldn't expect Mary to join me," Annie assured her. "But I have our birth Mamm's address here in Lancaster, and Mary should know before I contact our Mamm. And we—Mary and I—should meet each other. Don't you agree?" Annie's voice ended in a plea.

Rebecca appeared to waver. "And how do you have all this proof?"

Annie dug in her satchel and produced the papers. "These are from the Hope Clinic."

"And they gave these to you?" Rebecca scanned the papers quickly.

Jesse cleared his throat. "We obtained them yesterday through the help of the former director's daughter."

"They do have our names right here." Rebecca's face softened. "Mr. and Mrs. Lester Mast. It was before Lester was ordained to the ministry. We were young and childless. Like Hannah of the Scriptures, I prayed my heart out that the Lord would give us children. Even Lester thought the chance for us to adopt a child was a miracle. After we brought Mary home, I thought there would be more Kinner. There usually is in such cases, but I was never given one of my own." Tears trickled down Rebecca's face. "But we have Mary, and we love her with all our hearts."

"I'm sure you do," Annie agreed. "Can I please meet my sister?"

Rebecca paused, then finally opened the door fully. "Mary is upstairs. I will call her."

Annie glanced at Jesse while Rebecca hurried over to the stairwell. Jesse's look said that he agreed. They both knew that Amish girls didn't belong upstairs in the early-morning hours. Rebecca had sent Mary into hiding when they had pulled into the driveway.

"Mary?" Rebecca called up the stairs.

"Yah, Mamm," a weak voice answered.

"Come down. There is someone here to meet you."

Tentative footsteps soon followed.

Annie's heart pounded. What if Mary dashed upstairs again after she was told the news?

Mary—her twin sister—appeared in the stairwell, but stayed on the first step. "What is going on, Mamm?"

"This is Annie and Jesse." Rebecca motioned with her hand. "They have come with some news that might interest you. They just told me that you are not only adopted, but— " Rebecca was overcome. "I'm sorry, I can't speak right now."

Mary came down the steps and laid her hand on Rebecca's arm. "What is it? Tell me."

"You know that we love you," Rebecca whispered. "That will never change, and we would have told you if we had known."

Concern filled Mary's face. "What has happened?" she asked Annie.

"I am adopted too, Mary," Annie began. "I have been searching for my birth Mamm. In my journey, I have found out something that I didn't know growing up, and that neither of our parents knew. We are not only adopted, Mary. You and I are sisters, twins."

"Is this true?" Mary asked, this time directing the question to Rebecca.

A quick nod came. "I just saw the papers, Mary."

Annie opened her arms. "You know this is true, Mary. Deep

down this explains so much: the longing, the missing pieces, maybe even the same desire I have to meet our birth Mamm. Haven't you felt the same thing?"

Mary hesitated.

"You are my sister, Mary, my twin." The tears stung. "I know this may come as a terrible shock, but you must feel a little of what I do. Somehow I always knew."

Mary raced to Annie. They embraced and clung to each other while Rebecca sobbed beside them.

Jesse had tears in his eyes too, and Annie saw them as she let Mary go. She wanted to give him a hug—for sharing this moment with her, for being here, for not giving up hope until the break had come in the clouds–but she couldn't. Not in Bishop Mast's living room.

"Can we sit on the couch and talk?" Mary stepped back but took Annie's hand.

They seated themselves while Rebecca motioned for Jesse to join her in the kitchen. "Come help me rustle up something to eat while these two get acquainted."

Jesse smiled at Annie and followed Rebecca out of the room.

Mary was staring at her. "I have a twin sister. I can't believe this. You're right—I have always felt that a part of me was missing."

Annie nodded, her voice too choked at the moment.

"I'm trying to sort this out. You are here, and you are my twin sister. What is life like in Nebraska? That is where you are from, correct?"

Annie managed to laugh. "Not much different from Lancaster County—colder maybe, and more remote."

Concern rippled on Mary's face. "Daett had some things to say about your district being liberal."

Annie shifted on the couch. “I’m sorry we had such a difficult start. We didn’t know for sure if you were my sister when we arrived the other day. We hadn’t found our Mamm’s address yet.”

“Is she really here in Lancaster County?”

“That’s where the address is, but we don’t know if she still lives there. The paperwork is twenty-one years old. I wanted us to meet so I could tell you before I went there. I thought that maybe—”

“This is all so strange,” Mary mused. “I knew I was adopted, but I was happy. I guess I was not really thinking about things, and going on with my life. It never occurred to me to find my birth Mamm.”

“So you were also told?”

Mary nodded. “Not in long talks or that sort of thing. Mamm dropped hints, and so did others in the community. I knew, I guess, but maybe I didn’t want to know more.”

Annie reached for Mary’s hand. “But we are sisters. You must feel that?”

A hint of a smile crossed Mary’s face. “I do now, but I always tried to explain the longing away. I thought it was something else, I guess.”

“We have missed out on so much. We have so much to catch up on, so much to share. How we grew up, what our plans are for the future.”

Mary’s smile grew. “I’m to wed Ben Wengerd this fall and keep his house. Hopefully the Lord will bless us with many Kinner. I have always loved them.”

“So have I.” Annie squeezed Mary’s hand. “So you have found love? That’s something I never could quite give myself to until I found our Mamm.”

“Ben is wunderbah.” Mary’s eyes glowed. “He has forty acres in his name. That’s not bad for a start in Lancaster County. And

Daett approves. I think Ben is right for me."

Annie took a deep breath. "I hope I'm not disturbing your world by bringing you this news."

"Ben knows that I am adopted. He won't be upset that I have a twin sister. He will probably even welcome you as a sister-in-law."

"I'm so glad that you have found happiness."

"We can write, can't we? And you must come to our wedding this fall. Can you travel again from out in Nebraska?"

"Of course! It would be a great honor to attend your wedding. And yes, we can write. I can keep you up on the news about our Mamm."

Mary hesitated. "I don't know if Daett would like that. We can write about other things, and Daett won't object to you attending my wedding. I will tell him we must send you an invitation."

"Who will be the witness on your side of the family?"

Mary's face lit up. "You could be. How perfect!"

"Oh, I don't expect that! I'm just glad I can come to your wedding," Annie sputtered.

Mary wasn't deterred. "I won't hear anything else. By the way, your boyfriend is so handsome. I saw you from the upstairs window, leaning on his arm as you came up the walk this morning. You can sit beside me, and he can sit beside Ben." Mary clasped her hands in delight.

"Wait, wait. We aren't dating. We are just goot friends." Annie stopped. Protests were useless. Mary had seen them, and she wouldn't believe Annie's denials. If Mary knew that Annie had kissed Jesse yesterday, she would have wondered why Annie hadn't set her own wedding date.

"Just as you say," Mary said, with a mischievous glint in her eye. She changed the subject. "I'm going to wear a dark-blue dress. The bridesmaids' dresses will be a little lighter blue, but not much. Daett said pride is an awful thing and shows up most easily on wedding days, when great joy is in our hearts and we are not on guard."

Annie nodded and continued to listen. That Mary had been brought up differently became more obvious the longer they talked. But what did that matter? Mary was her twin sister, and they had found each other. If she had to find her birth Mamm on her own, that would be the Lord's will. She would not let life separate her from Mary again.

Out in the car, Lily jerked her head up when the barn door swung open and the bishop's form burst out into the sunlight. He barreled toward the car. Lily hunched down in the seat. Her words had been brave this morning, but now she must watch her words when she spoke to the bishop. Maybe the man would rush past her, where Jesse could handle him in the house.

Lily held her breath as the bishop slowed to peer into the car. He stepped closer and motioned for Lily to roll down the window. Lily tried, but the key was off and the button didn't work. The bishop thumped on the glass, his bearded face inches away.

Lily pushed open the car door and stepped out. "Hello, Bishop."

"Why are you back here?" he thundered. "What kind of Amish girl drives a car, or are the others with you?"

Lily bit back a quick retort.

"Can't you speak, child? The cat obviously got your tongue." The bishop's head jerked toward the house. "I'm thinking the rest of your gang is in the house with Mary at this moment. Is that what's going on?"

Lily let her breath out slowly. "We found proof that Mary is Annie's twin. Did you know this?"

The bishop whirled about. "I don't know what you are talking about, young woman. Adoption records are sealed. Everyone knows that."

"And yet I found them."

"You did? Well, I'll be! That changes everything, doesn't it?" he said sarcastically.

"You don't have to mock me, Bishop. I expected better of you."

The bishop's face flamed red. "I will not have you lecturing me about what is right and wrong. I already told you this. You are a woman, but obviously you don't know your place. What kind of parents do you have anyway?"

Lily raised her voice. "Goot, godly parents who taught me how to treat guests with kindness and respect."

"With a daughter like you," the bishop huffed, "it makes one wonder."

"You have some nerve!" Lily glared at him.

Behind them the front door of the house burst open and Jesse hurried down the walk.

Jesse slowed his rapid pace as he approached the Malibu. What would he say when he got there? Lily was glaring at Bishop Mast, and the bishop was glaring equally at her and at Jesse. Something must be said to defuse the situation. Maybe he had been wrong in not going to the barn first and speaking with the bishop. But that would only have provoked a reaction from the get-go, with a possible expulsion from the farm. Annie never would have gotten to speak with her twin sister.

"Goot morning, Bishop." Jesse forced a smile. He came to a halt before the two red-faced combatants. "I hope we haven't interrupted your work this morning with our arrival."

"My work!" the bishop bellowed. "It's my daughter I am concerned about, and the lies you are telling her. This woman right here—this bold woman, this—" The bishop's hand flailed in Lily's direction. "What falsehoods she spins."

"I'm afraid Lily is telling the truth, Bishop. We should go somewhere and talk calmly about this."

"What is wrong with the Lord's open heaven for this conversation?" The bishop appeared beside himself. "Or are you trying to hide things from the Lord's eyes?"

Jesse took his time to answer. "We're not trying to make trouble. But the truth is the truth and must be faced."

The bishop's mouth worked soundlessly for a moment. "The truth, young man! What do you know about the truth? I am a bishop, anointed of the Lord, and you are telling me what is the truth."

"I'm sorry for the way that sounded," Jesse said, trying to mollify the man. "But Annie is Mary's twin sister. We have the papers to prove it. Surely you would not keep family apart."

"Now you would lecture me!" the bishop roared. "How many times must I tell both of you that this will not work?"

Jesse moved back a step. An enraged bishop served no one's purpose, especially Annie and Mary's relationship. But what else was there to say? "I'll go get Annie and we will leave," he finally said.

The bishop didn't answer, his gaze fixed on the house.

Jesse turned to see Annie running toward them. She didn't stop until she was in the back seat of the car and had pulled the door shut behind her.

"I guess I won't need to get Annie," Jesse said. "We're leaving."

Lily beat him to the car and they drove slowly out of the lane.

Jesse glanced over the back of the seat. "What happened, Annie?"

Tears streamed down Annie's face. "Why did our first meeting have to end like that? Mary turned whiter than a ghost when she heard her Daett hollering out by your car."

"I'm so sorry about this," Lily whispered. "I tried to hold my tongue, but it did no goot."

"It'll be okay," Jesse told Annie. "Somehow."

He didn't know how, but he would do everything in his power to bring healing to Annie's broken relationships.

14

Soon after the sun came up the next morning, Annie sat at the kitchen table with Lily beside her and Jesse and Grandma Yoder across from them. The breakfast dishes were still unwashed and in disarray around them. From the kitchen window, the early-morning light streamed across the sink to spill over the vinyl floor. Annie moved her foot into the bright rays, and her black shoe shone.

If only life were that simple. If only there was some way to know how to move forward. A restless night of tossing and turning had produced few answers. Whichever way she looked, there was Bishop Mast's angry face, and any plans for her future relationship with her twin were doubtless out the window. Mary's sweet temperament in spite of the pressure she lived under was a marvel indeed.

"So what are we doing, other than sitting around moping?" Lily's voice broke into Annie's thoughts. "I don't see much sense in waiting. The bishop is not changing his mind. Annie will have to meet her Mamm by herself."

Jesse cleared his throat. "I'm afraid that even if we leave him alone from now on, Bishop Mast may make trouble for us. Is that not right, Grandma?"

His grandmother thought for a moment. "Well, we do live in another district, but an angry bishop is always a problem. He could make a call to a Nebraska Amish phone shack and bring Annie's search to a close—or try to at least."

Annie's sharp intake of breath was drowned out by Lily's encouragement: "Deacon Bontrager will stick up for us."

Annie let her breath out slowly. "Even if Deacon Bontrager would support us, it wouldn't be right to put the community through any more of my turmoil. They've already been through too much."

Jesse's smile from across the table warmed her. "I'm sure everyone in the community will try and be supportive now that we know we are on the right track. A girl's search for her Mamm is the right thing. They know this in their hearts."

"I agree," his grandmother added. "Now if someone could convince the bishop."

"I say we set out on our day's adventures," Jesse said. "Enough moping."

Annie stood. "Not until we wash the dishes. Duty comes first."

"Duty does come first, and your duty now is to find your Mamm. Go!" Grandma Yoder waved at the washroom door. "I can handle the dishes this morning. It keeps me young."

Laughter filled the kitchen, but Annie ignored the order and prepared a stack of dishes. When a further protest didn't come from Grandma Yoder, Annie looked up to see Lily peering out of the kitchen window.

"Who is it?" Annie asked.

Lily glanced over her shoulder. "I don't know. The buggy is just sitting there by the hitching rack."

"Who could it be?" Grandma Yoder began to rise from her chair.

Lily leaned farther over the sink. "It's Mary, your twin!"

Annie dropped the dishes with a clatter.

Jesse bolted out of the kitchen.

"You'd better go with him," Grandma Yoder told Annie.

Lily grabbed Annie by the arm and propelled her after Jesse, who was already out the washroom door. Halfway across the lawn he waited for the two girls to catch up, and together they approached the closed buggy door.

"Are you sure it is Mary?" Jesse asked Lily.

"I'm sure," Lily said. "And if we don't get there soon, she's going to drive off."

"That might be the best thing." Jesse glanced at Annie. "Sorry, I didn't mean that. Mary being here is goot, regardless of what happens with the bishop."

Annie took Jesse's hand and leaned against his shoulder. She had no right to draw comfort from him again, but he didn't object.

Annie focused on the closed buggy door that slowly opened to reveal Mary's tense face. Annie rushed forward and Mary leaped out of the buggy to cling to her. "I'm so scared, Annie, I really am, and yet I had to come. I hope you understand."

"Did you want to talk more about keeping in touch and about me attending your wedding? I'm sorry we didn't end things better yesterday."

"It's not that," Mary whimpered. "After Daett's hollering, I knew we couldn't continue on like we had been. I want to join in the search for our Mamm, Annie. All night I have been up thinking about it, and deep down I want to know. I must, even if Daett disapproves. He's going to disapprove of everything anyway."

"Does Ben know about this?" Jesse asked.

Mary's face grew paler. "Daett had Ben come over last night for supper and told him everything. Ben is afraid of Daett, I think. We weren't allowed to speak with each other alone before Ben went home. I know Ben would support me if I join you in a search for our Mamm. I can't cut off our relationship, Annie. Not after I have only just met you. You are my sister."

"The nerve of the man!" Lily exploded.

"Be careful," Jesse warned. "Mary is under enough stress."

Mary was shaking, but her jaw was set. "Let's go before my courage fails me. I'm not used to acting like this. My heart tells me I am right, but my mind is screaming how wrong I am for defying Daett. I really should go home before Daett finds out about this, but I can't. I must meet our birth Mamm. I came as soon as I could this morning, once Daett had gone to work in the back fields. Mamm understands and helped me hitch Ginger to the buggy."

Annie tugged on Mary's hand. "Come into the house, please. You are too distraught to leave right now. We can fix hot chocolate and talk. You'll feel better."

"I'll tie up the horse." Jesse already had the tie strap in his hand.

You had best unhitch, Annie mouthed to Jesse, and he nodded. Mary appeared ready to bolt. She trembled on the walk to the front door.

Grandma Yoder greeted them with a worried look. "Mary!"

"I am so sorry. Daett will be quite displeased when he finds out, but I can't help it. I want to meet my birth Mamm. Annie was right. She was right about so many things. More than I can say."

Annie guided Mary to the couch, and Lily hurried to the other side.

Grandma Yoder hovered about, clearly uncertain what should be done.

"I'll go make hot chocolate," Lily said and vanished into the kitchen. Grandma Yoder followed.

With Grandma Yoder hovering at her shoulder, Lily heated the pan of milk over the open flame, listening to the soft murmur of the voices coming from the living room. Jesse was still outside in the barn, probably filling in his grandfather on the details of Mary's sudden arrival.

Mary hadn't run away from home, but she had sneaked off without Bishop Mast's approval. She couldn't imagine the bishop's furor when he found out. The man would see it as a serious embarrassment. There would be no resolution until Mary returned home. They should leave immediately, but Mary was in no shape to venture out on a search for the twins' Mamm. On the other hand, leaving the girl with Jesse's grandmother would negate Mary's courageous action. They would just have to wait until she calmed.

Heat rose from the milk and Lily stirred it slowly with her spoon. Grandma Yoder had the cocoa powder out on the countertop, with several cups near at hand. A troubled expression lingered on Grandma Yoder's face.

"It's quite a fix we are in, isn't it?"

Grandma Yoder nodded.

"How will this affect you?"

Grandma Yoder hesitated. "I don't know. Depends on what happens. We didn't ask Mary to visit."

"But you are allowing her to stay."

"That's the rub."

"Mary is old enough to make up her own mind, isn't she?"

Grandma Yoder winced. "There is the bishop, of course. That sort of changes things, and the girl is promised to Ben Wengerd."

Lily concentrated on the pot. If she burned the milk the day would only get worse.

"We could ask the girl to go back home," Grandma Yoder mused. "If she says no, the matter is out of our hands, but that would be cruel. Mary does have the right to meet her birth Mamm. And it would be cowardly to make sure she takes all the heat for this."

"After we have found their Mamm, we could pick up Mary for a visit. Sneak her out again."

Grandma Yoder snorted. "That won't happen. Once Mary is home, Bishop Mast will see that she stays there. Rebecca is probably getting a tongue-lashing right now. The woman won't dare to help Mary with this again."

"Confound the bishop," Lily snapped.

"Careful," Grandma Yoder warned. "The man is anointed of the Lord to watch over his people. He's a little zealous, but better that than too lax."

Lily leaned over the pan. The milk didn't need to boil, but the right temperature was difficult to achieve.

"Can I have a sampling spoon?" Lily asked.

Grandma Yoder produced one with a flourish, and Lily tested the milk. "This is ready."

Lily stepped back and Grandma filled the cups with milk. The powder had been added earlier and swirled near the top. Grandma stirred it in, a worried look still on her face.

Jesse poked his head through the washroom door. "Is the coast clear?"

"Annie and Mary are in the living room, talking."

Jesse came in the rest of the way. "That's why I didn't go in there, but I was afraid I'd find them in the kitchen."

"I'm sure Annie wants you with her," his grandmother assured him.

"I don't know." Jesse sighed. "Everyone is on edge at the moment. How in the world is Bishop Mast going to react?"

His grandmother's smile was grim. "What did your grandfather have to say?"

"I couldn't find him in the barn. He must be back in the pasture, looking after the cows."

"I wish he was up here." Grandmother paused with a plate of cups in her hands. "But that can't be helped. Are you two coming?"

"Hot chocolate?" Jesse made a face. "There are limits."

"Comfort drink," Lily explained. "Right now we need all the help we can find."

"Well, that's true," he muttered.

"Cheer up. Joy will come in the morning," Lily said brightly.

No one laughed.

Lily hung back as Jesse disappeared with his grandmother into the living room. She wanted to join them, but Annie was overwhelmed as it was. Besides, if Annie needed anyone, it was Jesse, and Lily must not be bitter. She had to accept the truth. With how Jesse responded to Annie, she could never imagine that he would someday return her affections. Jesse and Annie had a connection of the heart. Annie hadn't set out trying to win the man, but she had.

This was an impossible situation.

"Why aren't you in the living room with us?" Jesse asked, and Lily jumped.

"Why did you come back?" she retorted. "Annie needs you."

He smiled. "I appreciate how you stood up to Bishop Mast, Lily."

She glared at him. "You were the one hushing me."

"I still admire your fire."

"Thanks," she said, wishing those words could be enough for her.

He smiled. "You have been goot for Annie on this trip. We'd already be at a dead end if you hadn't found a way into the Hope Clinic."

"We also wouldn't be having this ruckus right now."

"That would have happened either way. You know it."

Lily hung her head. "I suppose so, but my tongue is too sharp."

"You have been a goot sister. You want Annie and now Mary to find their birth Mamm, and you don't like how the bishop runs things."

"Agreed," she allowed.

He took on a musing tone. "Mary shares Annie's beauty. You can tell they are twins right away."

Lily looked away. His words cut, though Jesse didn't intend them to. He spoke only the truth. Annie was pretty.

Jesse was looking at her. "I didn't intend to . . . to imply that you are not pretty. You know that, don't you?"

She tried to smile, and her tone was dry. "Oh yes, I'm a raging beauty."

He grinned. "You should have plenty of chances to wed. That is, if you want to."

I want to wed you. The words almost came. Maybe she should blurt them out, shout her feelings from the rooftops, but that wouldn't work with Jesse.

"I'm also thankful for what you are doing on Annie's behalf," she told him.

He smiled and nodded before he left through the washroom again.

An hour later Jesse sat on the front porch swing. He swung slowly to the soft creak of the chains above him. He had snuck out through the washroom door after his conversation with Lily. He should have gone into the living room, but the three women were best left alone at the moment. Annie might want him with her, but the distraught Mary would respond better to a woman's touch. What Mary must live through under the zealous bishop's care boggled his mind. From the appearance of things, freedom had always been a scarce commodity.

The front door squeaked, and Jesse looked up to see Annie step out of the house. He leaped to his feet, but she motioned for him to sit. "I want to join you, if that's okay. I saw a glimpse of you through the window."

Jesse lowered himself again. "How are you doing? Is Mary okay?"

"Resting." Annie appeared tired. "We'll let her sleep until lunch.

The poor girl was up all night. She didn't exaggerate on that point."

"Is she still planning on joining us on our search?"

Annie nodded. "We should visit that address after lunch. Mary will still be tired, but if we could get her back by tonight, that would probably be best . . ." Annie's voice trailed off.

"Wise thinking," Jesse agreed. "What if your Mamm is really there?"

Annie glanced at him. "I don't know. I guess we'll have to explain things, complicated and strange as they are. And I can go back the next day, and the day after. I can't just rush back to Nebraska if I find her. Not after these long years."

"Of course," he said, taking her hand.

Annie's fingers tightened around his. "You are so understanding. How can I thank you enough, or even think of repaying you?"

He shook his head. "Let's just find your Mamm and get Mary back before the world comes crashing down on our heads."

"You think it will be that serious?"

"You know it will be."

Annie looked away. "Listening to Mary talk, I have to say you are right. I guess I was trying to convince myself. We are playing with fire."

"Did you ever think you would have to walk through all this?"

"No, but I have found my sister. That was worth the trouble we have already been through, and the trouble we have yet to face."

"We will find your Mamm," he said, and Annie leaned against him.

They swung slowly, the chains squeaking above them. He wanted to hold her, kiss her again. But first the road ahead must be traveled.

Jesse breathed a quick prayer heavenward. *Please let this work, Lord.*

15

Around one o'clock that afternoon, the kitchen table at the home of Jesse's grandparents was strewn with the remnants of a hurried lunch: homemade dressing for a salad with homegrown tomato chunks, ham, butter, and a partially cut loaf of bread. A prayer of thanks had been offered by Grandpa Yoder ten minutes ago, but no one had left the table.

Annie gave Mary a quick glance. The kitchen must be cleaned before they could leave, but Mary's face was white as a sheet. She had seen Mary eat during their hearty meal, so that was not the problem.

"Are you okay?" Annie nudged Mary.

Her twin managed a nervous smile. "I think so. I'm just jumpy." Mary's face twitched. "Daett will be very upset."

"Do you think that your Daett might come here?" Annie asked.

"I don't know. He might." A tear trickled down Mary's cheek. "I don't think Daett would, but he could have gone over to speak with Deacon Beiler. If Daett did, the deacon is on his way here . . ." Mary's voice faded out.

Annie stood. "We have to clean the kitchen, then go. We can't take the chance."

As one they followed her lead. Lily ran water in the kitchen sink, and the kitchen was spotless fifteen minutes later.

Grandpa Yoder disappeared into the washroom, and the outside door creaked shut behind him. A moment later he was back with a worried look on his bearded face. "I know you were trying to get away, but we have a visitor."

They stared at him.

"It's not Bishop Mast." Grandpa Yoder leaned on the doorknob. "Deacon Beiler, I think. Mary guessed right."

"We must go talk with him." Grandma was the first to speak.

"I'll bring him in." Grandpa Yoder turned to go. "That would be better."

"Maybe not," Grandma Yoder protested.

Mary clung to Annie while Grandpa went out the washroom door again, his shoulders stooped.

"What do you think the deacon wants?" Jesse asked.

No one answered. But they all knew. Amish deacons visited to enforce the Ordnung or other dictates from the bishop.

"Come." Grandma Yoder took Mary's arm. "Let's go sit on the couch."

Annie joined her. Together they ushered the trembling Mary to the living room. The girl moaned with each step. "Daett will have me excommunicated for sure! Why else would he have sent Deacon Beiler?"

"Excommunication takes awhile," Jesse said, trying to comfort her.

"Hush!" Lily said. "She's not going to be excommunicated."

Mary appeared to be on the verge of hyperventilation.

"Shall I get a paper bag from the kitchen?" Lily asked.

"Mary will be okay." Grandma Yoder forced a smile. "We don't want to make more of a fuss than necessary."

Stooped forms passed the living room window in front of them. Deacon Beiler didn't appear much younger than Grandpa Yoder, his white beard stretching down his chest. Surely the man would have some understanding of the situation. Maybe he had even raised daughters of his own.

The front door opened and Grandpa Yoder led the way inside.

Deacon Beiler took off his hat and approached. "Mary," he said gently, "what are you doing here?"

"I—I'm . . ." Mary's voice failed her.

"You should be at home," Deacon Beiler continued. "Your Daett has gone to tell Ben of your whereabouts."

Mary shivered.

"Can I take you home?" Deacon Beiler held out a hand. "Come. I'm sure this can be explained to your Daett as a moment of weakness, and Ben will certainly forgive you. It is understandable that you would wish to meet your birth Mamm, but this is not a wise choice. You can't risk what the Lord has given you in the community for what the English world offers out there."

"She's my Mamm." Mary found her voice.

"And your birth Mamm is also English, and gave you up for adoption." Deacon Beiler's hand was still outstretched. "Let's go home, Mary."

"I can't," Mary whispered.

"Of course you can. I will help you down the steps and into the buggy. There will be peace at home once you give up this foolishness."

Annie stifled a protest. Her words would not help Mary's situation. Her twin needed to arrive at her own decision. Lily had disappeared into the kitchen, apparently in an effort to control her temper. Jesse took a quick look around and followed Lily.

Annie kept her hold on Mary's hand as the deacon continued. "I know these may be hard words to hear right now, but in the end you will see the wisdom of what I'm saying. Come." The deacon held out his hand again.

Mary pulled back. "I'm not coming. My decision is made."

Deacon Beiler looked around. "Who influenced you in this rebellion? This is not the Mary I know. Mary Mast has always been a submissive and obedient woman."

Color crept into Mary's cheeks. "I have a right to meet my birth Mamm."

"What have they been telling you?" Deacon Beiler's accusing gaze took in both Annie and Grandma Yoder.

"We have not been telling her anything, Deacon," Grandpa Yoder said calmly.

"Then these people from Nebraska have been?" Deacon Beiler glared at Annie. "What tales have you been telling the girl?"

Annie didn't know what to say.

"Someone has been teaching Mary rebellion!" Deacon Beiler declared. "When you came to speak with Mary, the first seeds of this rebellion must have been sown."

"Going on a search for one's birth Mamm is not rebellion." Annie found her voice.

"So you are the one to blame." Deacon Beiler's gaze settled on Annie.

Mary perched on the edge of the couch. "I am to blame, Deacon, and no one else. I'm not coming home with you until I have met my birth Mamm. She lives right here in Lancaster County, so I should be home by tomorrow. You can tell Daett that. I know that Ben will understand. He is close to my heart, but much too afraid of Daett."

Deacon Beiler stroked his beard for a long time before he turned to Grandpa Yoder. "You have heard what everyone is saying, so I will say no more, but this cannot go on. The bishop wants his daughter home, and so does the man to whom she is promised. I expect you to stand with us on that decision and see that Mary is returned before nightfall. Maybe she will listen to your wisdom. If not, other steps will be taken." Deacon Beiler yanked his hat onto his head and headed out of the front door with Grandpa Yoder close behind him. His buggy wheels soon rattled out of the driveway.

The living room was silent. Lily clasped and unclasped her hands while she paced the kitchen floor.

Jesse stood by the window with his arms folded. "The deacon's gone."

Lily still paced. "What are we going to do?"

"What are my grandparents going to do? That would be the better question."

Lily paused with a start. "You don't think they will throw us out?"

Jesse shrugged. "It wouldn't be right to continue to impose on them after what we just heard, even if they still support us."

"But . . . but . . . ," Lily sputtered. "This is outrageous."

"The community back home isn't that supportive of Annie's venture," Jesse reminded her. "What happens if they hear of this?"

"At least it's not Annie who is forbidden to continue her search." Lily's hands flailed in the air.

"Neither is Annie a bishop's daughter, who is promised to become someone's Frau. They don't want their cozy world upended."

"But Mary just wants to find her Mamm." Lily's voice rose higher. "Like Annie does, and after that Mary will return home. What is so wrong with that?"

"You know where this could lead."

"Then what are we going to do?"

"We should talk with the others." Jesse motioned toward the living room.

Lily turned and Jesse followed her. Annie had her arms around Mary on one side while Grandma Yoder held her on the other. Mary sobbed quietly between them.

"That was so brave of you," Lily said.

Mary glanced up for a moment before she buried her face in her hands. In front of them the door opened and Grandpa Yoder walked in. He eased himself into his rocker with a groan. "What a day! And the deacon is serious, I think."

"We are not doing anything wrong." Grandma Yoder let go of Mary. "I hope you're not thinking that."

Grandpa sighed. "This is not up to us or what we think. You know that."

Grandma Yoder's face was sober. "What a horrible choice it leaves us."

"I don't think Bishop Mast is right, but no one is asking me," Grandpa Yoder said helplessly.

"Isn't there someone we can appeal to?" Lily asked. "You have other bishops in the community."

Grandpa Yoder shook his head. "That won't change Bishop Mast's mind."

"Then we will go over to Bishop Mast and talk sense to the man," Lily stated.

Mary's head shot up, and she stared at them with wide, horrified eyes.

"See," Grandpa Yoder said. "That makes my point. Mary knows her Daett best, and he's not changing his mind."

"We should still try," Jesse said from the kitchen doorway. "And we shouldn't stay here any longer, at least until this is resolved."

"I wasn't saying you have to leave," his grandfather told him.

"I know, but we both understand how this works. You have done enough."

Annie nodded and helped Mary to stand. "We should get packed and take everything with us."

"But what if we can get our bishop's support in Nebraska after we explain things?" Lily wouldn't give up.

But the others moved upstairs with Annie in the lead. There wasn't much to pack on Mary's behalf. The girl had fled from home with only a satchel. Lily and Annie's packing took a little longer.

Jesse was waiting outside in the hall when they left the room. He silently led the way down the stairs. They gathered in the living room, where Jesse addressed his grandparents. "Thank you so much for everything you have done. We will always appreciate your efforts and your kindness, and when this is over I promise I will visit again."

There were hugs and handshakes. Lily clung to Grandma Yoder for a long time. She wanted to whisper, "We will be back by evening," but even her courage had begun to fade. Now they really were on their own.

Annie helped Mary out of the house and down the front steps. Lily and Jesse followed with the luggage. Jesse's grandparents came out on the porch behind them. They stood arm in arm while Jesse opened the trunk. Annie and Mary got into the back seat. The twins waved goodbye through the back glass as they drove out of the lane. No one spoke until Jesse pulled into the small gas station and parked. He offered his cell phone to Lily. "Do you want to make the call?"

"I will." Annie spoke up from the back seat.

"That would be the best, I suppose. I might lose my temper," Lily agreed.

They waited while Annie climbed out and walked under the awning of the small station building. Annie turned her face away as if she wished to hide disappointment once someone answered at the phone shack—if anyone did. There was always a chance no one would be around. Annie was talking though, her head down, so someone must have picked up.

Mary whimpered in the back seat. "I wish I could be brave like Annie is. Like you all are. I'm so afraid."

"You are quite brave," Lily told her. "I heard you stand up to Deacon Beiler."

"You really were brave." Jesse sent Mary a warm smile. "You're still with us, aren't you?"

Mary wiped away a tear. "I just can't see how this is so wrong. And I know Ben feels the same way."

"We understand," Lily said kindly. "We really do. You are not doing anything you should be ashamed of."

Mary blinked back the tears and tried to smile.

Jesse kept his gaze on Annie. He should be by her side. She had turned toward them, and from the look on her face the news from Nebraska wasn't goot. But what did he expect? No one would dare go against the edicts of Lancaster County's conservative bishop, especially when his daughter was involved.

They hadn't kidnapped Mary, but he imagined it would feel about like this if they had.

Jesse looked up and saw that Annie's face was troubled as she approached the car and climbed into the back seat.

"What is the news?" He turned to face her.

Tears glimmered. "Seems that Bishop Mast has already called out to the community."

"I can't believe this!" Lily exclaimed.

Annie nodded. "Cousin Nancy didn't know much, but Deacon Bontrager was out to our place this morning. That can only mean one thing. Bishop Mast has already contacted the community, and you know what that means."

"It could have been a coincidence," Lily said.

Jesse shrugged. "Maybe, but my guess is Annie's right. What do you think, Mary?"

The girl's face was white as a sheet again and she was speechless.

"There's our answer." Jesse settled back into the seat.

"But we should make certain," Lily insisted.

Jesse glanced at Lily. "Who could you call who would know for sure?"

"Deacon Bontrager's phone shack is within hearing distance of the house," Lily said. "That must be how Bishop Mast made contact, and the deacon probably isn't home at the moment."

Jesse realized what she meant. "I like that. His Frau will answer. Do you know the number of the phone shack?"

"I only know ours," Lily told him, and Annie nodded.

"There must be a way," Jesse muttered.

He entered the town name into his smartphone and searched the Web with Deacon Bontrager's name added. The number came up on the first page. He dialed.

"How did you do that?" Lily asked.

He gave her a quick smile and listened to the ringing phone.

A woman answered at the fifth round. "Hello."

"Ah, hello," he responded. "This is Jesse Yoder, calling from Lancaster County. I'm with Annie and Lily Miller."

"Yah."

"Is Deacon Bontrager around?"

"No, he's out on his church rounds."

"Can you tell me if it's true that Bishop Mast contacted your husband—"

"Jesse," her voice interrupted him. "You know better than to ask me like that. You've been gone for a while, but you still know how we do things."

"That's why I'm asking you." He tried to chuckle. "I want to persuade Deacon Bontrager on the wisdom of what we are doing."

"You have Bishop Mast's daughter with you?"

"I do." Jesse held his breath.

"Then you had best take her back as soon as you can." Her voice was firm. "This is playing with fire, even if you are not a church member.

Your record will be tainted by this action. This has gone far enough. We thought Annie was looking for her Mamm, which was dangerous enough, but now you have dragged Bishop Mast's daughter into this. You have taken a promised woman from her home and tempted her with the things of the world."

"That was not our intention, but I am sorry that's how it looks," he said. "And I thank you for sharing your feelings with me. Tell the deacon I called and that we are in Lancaster County. Goodbye." He hung up.

"Well?" Lily asked.

"We are on our own. We will find a reasonably priced motel for the night and continue in the morning," he said and pulled out of the parking lot.

16

Annie awoke with a start. Where was she? In the dim light, the drapes on the windows were obviously those of a motel room. Annie rubbed her eyes. The familiar form of Lily was beside her, and across the room another girl was sleeping in another bed. *Mary!* Now she remembered. They were in a small motel near Lancaster.

Annie slipped out of bed and pushed back the drapes to peer outside. What time was it? In front of her, the dawn was written on the horizon with a bubble of growing light. The habit of waking early on the farm had followed her into the motel room of a strange English town.

"What time is it?" Lily's sleep-laden voice drifted through the air.

Annie let the drapes drop from her fingers. "Too early to get up."

Lily sat up in bed. "Must be about morning."

"You'll wake Mary," Annie warned.

Lily pushed back the bedcovers and swung her feet out onto the floor. Mary stirred in the bed across the room.

"See?" Annie said.

"I'm getting ready for breakfast." Lily headed for the bathroom.

Mary propped herself up on the pillows. "Where are we?"

"In a motel."

Mary rubbed her eyes. "Did I really do what I think I did yesterday?"

"Are you having regrets?" Annie sat on the bed beside her sister.

"No. I couldn't live with myself if I hadn't come with you. Daett would never give his permission for me to meet my English Mamm, and I didn't want to wait until I was married."

"At least you have Ben on your side." Annie forced a smile. "Of course we haven't found our Mamm yet. You might have to go home empty-handed."

"That would be awful." Mary shifted on the bed.

"But you have Ben to comfort you."

A wistful smile played on Mary's face. "I wish Ben would stand up to Daett."

Annie shook her head. "Maybe not. You know what that might mean."

Mary buried her face in her hands. "I know. Daett would forbid our wedding and that would be a complete mess. Even worse than the one I am in now."

"See, we are doing the right thing. Shall we straighten the room, so we can be ready to leave for breakfast?" Annie stood. "The food won't be much compared to what Grandma Yoder would have fixed for us."

"I'm sure that's true, but we couldn't put that kind of decision on them. This is our journey, and we must bear the consequences."

Annie smiled at her twin. "I couldn't agree more."

"What if I don't want to go back and face Daett?" Mary asked. "Once we find our real Mamm."

Annie tried to breathe evenly. "I don't think that is much of an option, do you? I mean, you have to go home."

"But you have thought that as well?"

"I think everyone has," Annie demurred. "Why do you think they are so worried? And the truth is neither you nor I knows what is ahead of us."

"Do you think we will want to stay with her if we find her?"

"There's no way to know. We just have to trust the rightness of our journey. Look, we have found each other. Think about that. We are sisters, twins. This search must be right."

"I know! One forgets in the kerfuffle."

"We should have known each other a long time ago."

"So the pain isn't too much for you?" Mary asked. "Do you wish you didn't know about me?"

"Mary!" Annie scolded. "Don't say things like that. Of course I don't regret knowing you."

"Even if we don't find our Mamm?"

The tears stung. "I will never regret meeting you, Mary. We have the years ahead of us. We know each other now, and nothing can change that."

"Not even Daett," Mary muttered darkly. "I'm not going back until I have found an answer, and even then Daett will have to deal with the fact that I have changed. This has made me different, just knowing that I have an English Mamm and a twin sister."

Annie searched for a response. What was the right thing to say? She was saved from answering when Lily came out of the bathroom.

"Next," Lily said. "Let's keep moving."

Annie glanced at Mary. "You can go first."

Mary nodded and grabbed her satchel.

"So what do you think?" Lily asked from the window drapes, peering outside.

"I guess I'm still trying to wrap my mind around the idea of meeting my real Mamm. I think we are close."

Lily glared out into the street. "I thought I would never see what I saw yesterday. What is wrong with Bishop Mast?"

"Mary is their only daughter."

"That's no excuse. It makes you question everything when people act like that."

Annie hurried to her sister's side. "Surely you aren't also entertaining thoughts of leaving the community. You are the strong one, Lily."

Lily moved away from the window. "I suppose not. I am Amish. Everyone knows that."

Annie's gaze lingered on her sister as Lily rummaged in her suitcase. Was Lily having doubts about her life in the community? Lily was unattached, but surely she wouldn't make that drastic step. Annie couldn't add further to the sorrow in the Miller family by influencing Lily to leave the faith. Her own troubles had been enough of a grief to Mamm and Daett.

"How do we get Jesse up?" Lily snapped the suitcase shut.

"I guess we call him on the phone."

"What phone?"

"The one on the desk there. Jesse's room is 202."

"And you know this how?"

"I remembered from last night. Our room is 210."

"I meant how to call him."

Annie shrugged. "I don't know. Maybe I heard others in the community talking about their travels."

Lily gave Annie a sharp look. "You are English. That's how you know."

"That's just silly. I don't have innate knowledge of English things. I was raised Amish." Annie sat on the bed. "Must we quarrel? We are still sisters, and you are imagining things."

Lily snorted. "You can't blame me for being affected by this. Bishop Mast's antics have my system in shock."

Annie searched for a response, but the bathroom door opened and Mary came out.

"How is this done?" Lily asked from the nightstand.

"Lift the phone and dial 202."

Lily did and a startled look crossed her face. "Jesse? Are you up?" There was a pause. "We want to eat soon . . . No, it's not too early—we can't sleep." Then, finally: "In twenty minutes then? Okay, we'll meet you at the car."

Lily hung up the phone and motioned to Annie. "Let's hurry. He wants to leave for breakfast in twenty minutes. They open at six."

Annie selected her clothes from the suitcase and hustled into the bathroom. She hadn't had the chance to warn Lily about her anger with Bishop Mast. Bitterness was never goot. Lily knew that, and surely she would come to her senses. If Annie and Mary jumped the fence to be with their English Mamm, there would be logic behind those decisions, but not for Lily. Annie would never forgive herself if the search for her birth Mamm caused that catastrophe.

An hour later, Lily led the group out of the fast-food restaurant. Her egg-and-bacon bagel had been okay, but it had been a poor substitute after several days of Grandma Yoder's cooking—one more bitter thought that swirled in her mind when she had too many already.

Jesse's car beeped ahead of them as he unlocked the door. Lily climbed in. She waited while Annie helped Mary into the back seat. This temper fit over Bishop Mast made her downright unsociable, when by nature she wasn't like that.

"You okay?" Jesse asked, sliding behind the wheel.

"Yes."

He raised an eyebrow.

"Thinking about yesterday," she finally admitted. "Bishop Mast."

"Some bishop," Jesse grunted. "Everyone has them though, even out in Nebraska. Or people like him, even if they aren't bishops. You know that."

Lily turned away. "I guess so, but it doesn't feel like I know it."

His touch was light on her arm. "It'll be all right. Tomorrow things will look better. We are about to find Annie and Mary's Mamm. Don't harbor bitterness."

She glared at him.

"I was out there. You don't want to do what you're considering."

How did he know I'm thinking about jumping the fence?

His hand lingered on her arm. Not that long ago she would have given almost anything to feel his touch. Now here they were, and she felt nothing. What a mess things were in.

Jesse pulled his hand away and started the car. "Everybody have enough to eat?"

The question was rhetorical. No one answered as he pulled out of the parking lot. They drove south away from town, and silence filled the car. Lily focused on where they were going. Was this the moment? The end of Annie's search? After these long years? *How do you walk up to a door and face the woman who gave birth to your adopted sister?*

Maybe she should go first, with Jesse by her side, and leave Annie and Mary in the car. The shock would be less to both parties. The crying would come later, and the hugs, unless they were turned away. She didn't want to think about that. Surely Annie and Mary's Mamm would see the twins. No mother who gave away her babies would refuse to do that.

Jesse slowed as they drove through a small suburb, the houses closer together and the streets narrow. She searched the house numbers with him. Annie and Mary were huddled together in the back seat, with only brief glances outside. Lily was sure they didn't really see any of the houses passing by.

"There it is," Jesse muttered, and he parked the car along the street. "Shall we?"

"Why don't you and Lily go first?" Annie's weak voice spoke from the back seat.

"I agree." Lily opened the car door and hopped out.

Jesse came around the car and they headed up the sidewalk together. He knocked. There was no answer for a long time, and Lily had just lifted her hand to knock a second time when the door opened.

An elderly man peered out at them. "Yes, may I help you?"

"I'm Lily Miller." Lily smiled her brightest. "We're looking for an Alisha Mandarin who used to live here."

"Alisha Mandarin? Never heard of her. Have you, Molly?" he called this last over his shoulder.

A woman appeared with a cane in her hand. "Who are you looking for?"

"Alisha Mandarin," the man said. "She used to live here."

Molly shook her head. "We moved to the house ten years ago to retire. Bernice Sanders, though, might know. She lives next door. Seems to me Bernice has lived here most of her life."

"Thank you." Lily stepped backward. "You have been very helpful."

"She's in that house." The man pointed.

They left him standing in the doorway, watching them leave. He was still looking when they reached the next sidewalk and approached the front door.

Lily knocked this time, and the door was answered quickly.

"Goot morning," Lily greeted the woman.

Bernice scrutinized them before she returned the greeting. "What can I do for you?"

"We are looking for Alisha Mandarin, who used to live next door."

"Alisha Mandarin." Bernice grew pensive. "That was many years ago. What could you want with her?"

"Her twin daughters are out in the car." Lily motioned over her shoulder.

Bernice lost some of her color. "You are sure about this?"

"We have papers to prove it."

"And how did you come by any such papers?"

"Long story." Lily produced the sheets. "See for yourself."

Bernice read them quickly. "Where you got these I can't imagine."

"They are correct, aren't they?"

"Why don't you get the twins and come in," Bernice said, "and we can discuss this on the living room couch instead of on the front porch."

Two minutes later Jesse helped Annie out of the car, while Lily did the same for Mary on the other side.

"This is not your Mamm, but she seems to know something of her," he told them.

Neither Annie nor Mary asked questions on the walk to the house. Bernice came out on the front step to meet them. "And you are?" She held out her hand.

"Annie Miller and Mary Mast." Jesse made the introductions.

"You knew our Mamm?" Mary whispered.

"I did. Let's go inside." Bernice led the way and seated them in her spacious living room. "I can't believe I'm seeing Alisha's daughters. Well, I suppose it was bound to happen. Such things do. We can't bury the past, you know."

"What was our Mamm like?" Annie asked. "Do you know where she lives now?"

Bernice smiled. "One question at a time. I have all day for Alisha's girls. So to the first one. What was your Mamm like?" Bernice settled back into the chair. "She was a darling—petite, cute as all get-out—but she got into trouble at a young age. Alisha wanted what was right, I know that much. That's why she put both of you up for adoption. We weren't that close, but being next door our lives crossed, and I know. I helped out during her pregnancy when I could. I figured I'd offer to babysit once you arrived in the world, but things never came to that. Alisha moved soon afterward. Didn't tell me why, but I did have her address at one time." Bernice stood and found an old folder. "I keep my contacts. One gets older, you know, and one can never have too many friends." Bernice paged through the folder. "Here it is. Alisha Mandarin in Fort Wayne, Indiana. Shall I make a copy?"

"Yes, please," Mary said breathlessly.

Jesse held Annie's hand while they waited. Bernice wrote carefully and handed him the paper.

"Was my Mamm married when we were born?" Annie whispered.

"She wasn't." Bernice's smile didn't fade. "But I'm sure she loved both of you with all her heart. I often heard her during the pregnancy, out on her front porch in the evening, rocking and singing softly. Your mother cared a lot about you. I'm sure she wanted the best for both of you. If she gave you up, it was because she thought you would have better lives that way. I hope you find her, and I hope your meeting is a joyous one."

Jesse helped Annie stand. "We can't thank you enough for your help," he said.

"It's my pleasure." Bernice waved them on their way. "May God be with you. I'm sure He's very interested in the joining of broken hearts."

The twins were silent as they left. Lily stayed close to Mary's side, while Jesse did the same for Annie. They made it back to the car and climbed in.

Jesse settled behind the wheel. "Shall we drive part of the way yet today?"

"Just go," Lily told him.

17

The following morning the interstate highway through Pennsylvania stretched out in front of them. Annie sat in the back seat with Mary beside her. Silence filled the Malibu, except for the hum of the tires on the pavement. Even Lily and Jesse in the front seat appeared exhausted. Jesse had his gaze fixed on the road, while Lily studied the passing landscape.

So much had happened in the last few days: the discovery of Mary, the confrontation with her Daett, their ejection from the home of Jesse's grandparents, and now the news that they had to go somewhere else in their search. They didn't dare call home to Nebraska again. Mamm and Daett might demand they return Mary at once and abandon their search. Bishop Mast was not a man anyone wished to defy, wrong though the bishop had been.

Annie gave Mary a weak smile. "I'm so sorry about your Daett. You must be all torn up."

Tears trickled down Mary's cheek. The girl hadn't eaten a bite in the restaurant they'd chosen after leaving the motel, so they'd brought her meal with them. It sat in a bag on the seat between them.

"Your food is getting cold," Annie encouraged.

Mary wiped her eyes. "I know, but I can't eat right now. Maybe later."

"I admire your courage," Annie said soothingly. "We must find our Mamm."

"We must!" Mary's eyes blazed. "We have come too far."

"Our loved ones are afraid of what we might find."

"Yah, I know." Mary nodded vigorously. "I could have tried to explain again, but it would have been useless. I'm planning to return once we find our Mamm."

"Are you sure about that?" Lily asked from the front seat.

"Lily!" Annie protested. Doubts were the last thing they needed at the moment.

"Are you sure you want to go back to that kind of control?" Lily pressed. "That oppression? You know that's what you were living under with your Daett."

Annie glared at her sister. Why had Lily decided to make things worse?

Mary struggled to compose herself before she answered. "I know I didn't have a free life like you and Annie did, but I love my Daett and Mamm. Daett tries to live how he thinks the Lord wants His people to live, and Ben—what a gift he is. I do so love him."

"Where is he then?" Lily retorted.

"Lily," Annie chided. "That is enough."

"I want to know. Isn't it a fair question?"

"I used to think you were the stable Amish girl." Annie tried another tack. "Remember back in Nebraska? You kept the garden and made things grow. You were ready for the rest of your life with the community."

"The garden!" Lily snorted. "Why do you bring up the garden at a moment like this? My garden seems years ago. Another life, even."

"How the mighty have fallen," Jesse said quietly.

"What do you mean by that?" Lily snapped.

"You're thinking of jumping the fence."

"Don't put words in my mouth." Lily took several deep breaths. "I'm just upset, that's all. Thinking about how Mary has been raised and used."

"Do you know how things are out there?" Jesse tilted his head at the passing landscape. "I don't think you do. Slow down and deal with your anger."

"Maybe I don't." Lily settled back in her seat. "Sorry. I'm just blowing off steam, and showing my temper—something I didn't know I had."

"We all have tempers." Jesse smiled at her. "I wasn't trying to chew you out."

"Yah, you were. And for goot reason." Lily didn't appear mollified in the least. "There goes your image of me as an Amish girl: decent, steady, unflinching, unflappable Lily. Now I steal papers out of a health clinic and talk about jumping the fence."

"You didn't actually steal them," Jesse corrected. "You were given copies. That's different."

"But I took them, and that's the point." Lily stared at the rolling countryside as they raced along. "Who would have thought? I've come far from raising gardens. There's no question about that."

Jesse had a twinkle in his eye. "Come to think of it, back in our school days I could never imagine you snatching contraband through windows."

Lily attempted a laugh. "You never know what lies beneath the surface. Not until you stir it with a stick."

"Now that's not fair," Jesse said. "You are a steady and settled Amish girl. Nothing will change that."

"Says who?" Lily muttered, her gaze still fixed out of the car window.

Mary leaned toward Annie to whisper. "Are they sweet on each other?"

Annie tried to breathe evenly. "Lily has always cared for Jesse."

"And they are fighting?" Mary raised her eyebrows.

"It would seem so."

"People fight when they like each other."

Annie almost laughed. "Or maybe when they are resolving issues."

Mary was clearly confused, and further explanations would not help. If Lily or Mary had known that Annie had kissed Jesse only a few days ago, that Jesse had held her in his arms, that she had clung passionately to him, their good opinion of her would almost certainly vanish.

"Are you all right?" Mary leaned close to whisper again.

"I'm okay," she lied.

Which made no sense. Why would she not be okay when it came to Jesse? In spite of Lily's display of temper, Annie knew her sister was much better suited as Jesse's Frau.

"What was your childhood like?" Annie asked. "We haven't had much chance to talk."

Puzzlement flitted on Mary's face. "Happy, I guess. I was an only child, and spoiled, I imagine, because my parents were unable to have any Kinner of their own. That must be why Daett panicked later and made so many rules. Daett wanted me to marry the first man who came along, which I didn't agree to." Mary made a face. "Mark Stoll would not have been someone I could learn to love. He had red hair and was a farmer. Those are not disqualifications, but he wasn't Ben."

"Is Ben really afraid of your Daett?"

Mary nodded. "Not that I blame him. Daett is not easy to deal with, and you know what trouble Daett could create by forbidding our marriage. Ben is sweet, and he likes me. After we're wed, things will be different." Mary's smile grew. "Daett's influence won't be there. Not like it is now."

"Ben sounds like someone I could like."

"I'm sure you will. After all, we are twins."

"Yah, we are. I'm so sorry we couldn't share our childhood."

"We missed a lot," Mary agreed, "but things could have been worse. Our Mamm could have left us somewhere horrible."

Annie nodded. "That is true. What do you think your Daett will do if we don't find our Mamm?"

Mary shivered. "I don't want to think about that. He'll have me confess my sins in church, I'm sure."

"Your Daett would make you go through that humiliation?" Horror filled Annie's voice.

"He would have no choice if I return empty-handed. Not after the fuss he's made."

"Then we really must find our Mamm!"

Mary's nod was the only answer as the sound of tires on the pavement clicked in perfect timing.

After a quick lunch of more fast food, Lily settled into the front seat and glanced at Jesse. "Happy?"

He patted his stomach. "Full at least."

Lily waited while Jesse started the car and pulled out of the parking lot. "Are we okay? You and I?"

"We've always been okay." Jesse gave her a sweet smile.

"Don't tease me, Jesse. I'm serious. I had a meltdown earlier and you took the brunt of it."

"I'm okay." He turned left and sped up to merge onto the interstate.

Annie and Mary were talking in low tones in the back seat, obviously continuing to catch up on their lost childhood. The two had been inseparable in their brief sit-down at the restaurant, while she and Jesse had shared uncomfortable glances. Why couldn't she make meaningful contact with him? This was how things always went, most of it apparently her fault. Annie was the one who had captured Jesse's affections. That was plain to see, and she should be happy. She was happy, only hope didn't die easily. She would forgive Jesse anything, even his current interest in Annie, if he would change his mind and love her.

Lily took a deep breath and glanced over into the back seat. Annie and Mary were engrossed in their conversation. She turned back to

Jesse. "I wanted so much to have your attention when we were in school. Surely you know that."

He nodded. "I know, and I wasn't trying to avoid you or be cruel."

"Just not interested?" The question cut deep.

"Must we torture ourselves with the past?" he asked. "Things were what they were, and we were children. We didn't know what we were doing, especially me. I didn't mean to hurt you, but yah, I could have been kinder, paid you more attention. My coolness wasn't necessary."

Her smile was weak. "That's nice of you to say, but would it have made a difference?"

"We could have talked with each other, been friends. Would that have made you happy?"

Lily looked away. "Would you have been happy? That is the question."

He shrugged. "I enjoy talking with you."

"But you didn't."

"I was full of myself. I admit it. I thought . . ."

"Thought what?"

"That when I left for Rumspringa, that I'd probably never come back. That was my plan."

Her fingers tightened. "That was your only reason?"

"You didn't keep me. That's the important point. Can we live with that?"

"Did I bring you back?" She knew the light of hope must have been blazing in her eyes, but she didn't care.

"I never dreamed I'd find you single."

"But you did." Lily couldn't breathe.

He tried to smile. "There you were, with Robert seated beside you."

"Did your heart sink? Were you disappointed?"

"Lily!"

"I want to know. Please tell me."

"Okay. I felt nothing. I figured there would be others who were available who fit my new plans."

"You came back to be practical? Is that it?"

He nodded.

"And I'm practical?"

"See what I mean? Why must we dig this up?"

"It was never buried."

"Do you want a husband who marries you because you fit the template?"

"You would grow to love me, Jesse. I know you would."

"We should leave this alone." His voice was firm.

"All because I threatened to jump the fence earlier in the day." It wasn't a question.

"You are never going to jump the fence, Lily. You are Amish to the core. No one worries about that."

"Is that not what you want?"

"It is," he agreed.

"My temper then? Is that the problem?"

He glanced at her. "You want to settle? Do you really?"

Tears stung her eyes. "That's so unfair."

"I'm sorry," he whispered. "I really am. I'm not saying we can't ever—"

"Just not now," she interrupted. "Until you make up your mind about Annie?"

He looked away.

Lily bit her lip. "This is my temper again, Jesse. I'm sorry. I shouldn't have pushed like this, but I couldn't help it. I want to know, for once, how things really are between us."

"Now you know," he said. "Are we enemies?"

"I could never be your enemy."

"Even if . . ." He let the words hang full of meaning.

"Even if you choose Annie." She forced the words out.

"This is an awful conversation, Lily."

"I know, but I asked for it. I needed it."

"Robert would love you. Surely you know that."

"And you wouldn't?"

"That is enough." He gave her a sharp look. "I did things on Rumspringa. We haven't even talked about that."

"I don't care," she said through clenched teeth. "You came back. That's all that matters."

He let his breath out slowly. "It should matter."

"But it doesn't?"

"This is enough for now." His voice fell lower. "We will say no more. Hear me."

"I'm sorry," she whispered. "I was out of my place." A tear trickled down her cheek.

His hand found hers. "I want nothing but the best for you. I want what you want—a man who can love you with his whole heart. Okay?"

She nodded, squeezed his hand, and let go. She must let go. She must not hang on. Not any longer.

Later that evening Jesse paid the bill for the two motel rooms with his credit card. They had arrived at the outskirts of Fort Wayne too late in the day to set out on any serious search for Annie and Mary's Mamm. One didn't pull up to houses once darkness had fallen with questions about missing people.

He signed the paper. The rooms were at opposite ends of the motel, as he had requested. Lily and Mary had already left with the card for the girls' room. Annie lingered. Had she overheard his conversation with Lily?

"Thank you," Jesse told the attendant.

"Have a good night's rest." The woman smiled.

Jesse turned to find Annie at his elbow. "Can we sit a moment before I go?" she asked.

He nodded and followed Annie to the dining room down the hall. She slid into a chair and gave him a warm smile. "I can't thank you enough for what you are doing for Mary and me."

So you didn't hear? The words almost slipped out. "You are welcome," he said instead. "And now let's pray for success tomorrow."

"May the Lord grant us the desires of our hearts," Annie whispered.

"You and Mary have already been united. That is something."

"Mary will suffer greatly if our effort fails."

"I can only imagine."

How, exactly, didn't matter. Bishop Mast's angry face brought several options to the forefront.

"We couldn't have done this without you," Annie said. "I will repay you for the motel bills once we get back to Nebraska. It is my fault that we can't stay with family and friends."

He forced a smile. "Unforeseen obstacles, but we carry on. Did you and Mary get caught up with each other on the drive today?"

Annie gazed at the far wall for a moment. "Mary had such a different childhood. I didn't know how goot I had things."

"So you will be staying in the community regardless of how this turns out?"

She gave him a sharp look. "I can make no promises—you know that."

He studied the profile of her face, caught in thought—so troubled under the surface, and yet so beautiful. Why had he never noticed her beauty before he left the community for his Rumspringa—before he had a past that throbbed in his heart, a pain he might never live down?

She caught his look and smiled. "You have been very kind. I don't know how I will ever repay you."

A kiss would help, he almost teased. He wanted more: her heart, her affections, her hand in his for the long walk through life, but nothing could change his past.

"Good night," he said. "We have a long day ahead of us tomorrow."

She touched his hand for a second and was gone.

18

Early the following morning, the girls took their usual places in the car while Jesse finished up in the motel.

"I'll be out in a moment," he had told them at the front desk. "Have to check out. The car is unlocked."

They had eaten a light breakfast at the motel's dining room, complimentary with their night's stay. Annie had swallowed quickly, hardly tasting the food. There had been cold cereal, scrambled eggs, toast, bacon, and instant oatmeal. The toast was made with a toaster, which had taken forever, but she had waited. Breakfast was so much better with toast, which brought memories of home. They were still far from Nebraska, both in miles and in heart. Would things ever be the same again, even if they returned? Lily had said little since they had gotten out of bed in their motel room. *Did something happen between Jesse and Lily yesterday?* The two had been in deep conversation while she was occupied comparing childhood notes with Mary, but she had caught none of what they said.

Annie leaned forward. "Are you okay, Lily?"

Her sister's smile was tense. "Yah. Just thinking. Today might decide everything."

What did she mean by that? "You're not thinking seriously about leaving the community, are you?"

"I'm not jumping the fence," Lily said reassuringly. "That was my temper talking yesterday. I know that things can be much worse even than the life Mary has had. I am sorry for my outburst."

"That's okay," Mary spoke up. "I can understand perfectly. If I were in your shoes, I would say the same thing. Daett isn't always what he should be."

"So you are going back?" Lily turned around in her seat.

"Unless something changes my mind, which I doubt."

"That must be hard, especially if we don't find your Mamm here in Fort Wayne."

"Don't say that," Annie protested. "This *must* end well."

They fell silent when Jesse appeared in the motel door and approached the car. He hopped in and said brightly, "Off on the final leg of our journey. To a blessed and happy reunion between daughters and mother."

Annie stifled a groan. "Thank you, but we have been disappointed so many times. I am afraid to get my hopes up."

"I know," he agreed. "But we are so close. I can feel it."

Annie saw Lily give Jesse a quick smile as he pulled out of the driveway. Jesse hadn't responded, but he hadn't frowned either. Had Lily mended fences with Jesse? Had the two planned a return to the community—with a wedding perhaps—once this search came to a satisfactory end? Jesse and Lily would make the perfect couple. Her shared kisses with Jesse would fade into his memory along with his Rumspringa. Lily would never be associated with Jesse's past, while Annie doubtlessly reminded Jesse of what he had experienced out in the world.

Mary's hand slipped into hers and Annie turned to meet her twin's troubled gaze. "Do you think we will really find our Mamm today?"

"We must," Annie told her.

Hope was so close and yet so far away. Annie tried to be positive, but they had been here before—pulling up to a strange address, then being told their Mamm was long gone. Why wouldn't their Mamm move on? A woman who had put her girls up for adoption couldn't be expected to put down roots.

Jesse had punched in the address to State Street in Fort Wayne last night when they pulled into the motel parking lot. The GPS claimed they were ten minutes from their destination. Mary likely didn't know how to read the GPS, but Annie had become accustomed to its insistent directions on the long journey from Nebraska to Pennsylvania and now back to Indiana. Mary's hand tightened in hers. Annie knew her sister was experiencing the same emotions she was.

"What do you think she looks like?" Mary whispered.

"Like us, probably." Annie attempted a smile.

That made sense, but Mary asked for a different reason. Annie had heard the same question in her heart. Regardless of what Bernice had claimed, what mother could abandon her children and not be changed in unimaginable ways?

"She must have had her reasons," Mary said.

Annie nodded. "And goot ones." She must imagine the best. The Lord would not have placed the desire in their hearts to meet their Mamm if the woman hated them.

"Almost there," Jesse sang out from the front seat. He slowed the Malibu a block later and parked.

Annie climbed out of the car. Mary joined her and clung to her hand.

"We'll go first," Lily said. She turned on her heel and made for the front door.

Jesse left with Lily, walking up the sidewalk while Annie and Mary waited. It was better this way. If their Mamm was in this house, she should have time to collect herself before seeing their faces.

"Lord help us!" Mary moaned.

"He will. I know He will."

"If she doesn't live here—I can't take much more of this."

Annie didn't respond. Jesse knocked on the front door. She couldn't see who opened, but the door had moved. She looked away and leaned against the car. Mary held her upright.

"They are looking at us," Mary whispered.

Annie forced her eyes open. The woman on the front porch was young, much too young. She couldn't be their Mamm. Lily gestured to them, and the woman sent them a little wave. Annie's hand wouldn't move. Another dead end.

"That can't be our Mamm," Mary seconded her opinion.

Jesse and Lily were coming back now, and the woman was still on the front porch, waving. To Annie, she appeared apologetic, as if she wished she were their Mamm.

"The woman knows nothing." Jesse stopped in front of them. "I'm sorry."

"She hasn't heard of an Alisha Mandarin," Lily added. "We could ask the neighbors, I guess."

"Let's just go." Annie found her voice. "We have to admit the truth sometime. We are not going to find her."

The tears were streaming down Mary's face. "We can't leave, Annie. We can't."

Annie took her twin sister in her arms. "I'm so sorry. You are right. I can't become discouraged. There must be some way, but what?"

"We will ask the neighbors," Jesse decided. "Can you wait here?"

"We'll wait inside the car," Annie told him.

She helped Mary in and sat on the seat beside her. Her strength was gone, and yet she breathed. The forms of Jesse and Lily as they walked up to the next house were like dim shadows that moved.

"We must pray." Mary took her hand. "We must."

Annie nodded, and they bowed their heads together.

"We can't give up!" Lily declared as Jesse drove out of town an hour later. "We tried and it didn't work, but something else will."

"You're the positive one." Jesse gave her a quick glance.

She sent him a warm smile. "We have to be, for everyone's sake."

Jesse would know what that meant. They had worked as a team for the last two hours, and Jesse had appeared comfortable. That wasn't love, just friendship, which was apparently the depth at which Jesse wanted their relationship to exist. She would have to accept it, but that didn't change her feelings. She was selfish, yes, clinging to the faintest of hopes, but that was the way things were.

"Are you okay back there?" Jesse asked, sending the question over his shoulder.

There was a quiet "Yah" from both Annie and Mary. The two were in shock, and Lily couldn't blame them.

"If we could figure the woman out, maybe we would know what she did next," Jesse suggested.

"How are we going to do that? I'm not a psychologist, and neither are you."

"You are a woman. Think like one." He glanced into the back seat. "They aren't in any shape to think."

Lily gave him a glare. "That's expecting a lot."

"I have confidence in you." He sent her a wink.

Lily looked away. Jesse could be cruel, but he didn't mean to be. She would have to keep that in mind. Maybe Alisha Mandarin was the same way, a woman who had to do what would appear to be cruel while wanting the best for her babies. Such a woman would . . .

Lily whirled to face Jesse. "I've got it! She's hanging around Amish communities. Not the one she left her children in because she doesn't want to interfere or run across them by accident. But she wants to see what their world is like. She wants to know that what she did . . ." Lily searched for words.

"That what she did was best for them," Jesse finished for her. "She would want to know that she did the right thing, and the only way to do that would be to study the community she sent her babies into. You are right."

Lily glowed. "I know I am."

"What is it?" Annie asked from the back seat.

"I think we have figured out your Mamm," Lily told her.

"You have?" both girls asked in unison.

Lily ran through the theory. "I'm thinking she would have married a man who would settle down near the community and not want to move again. That means your Mamm is close."

Neither Annie nor Mary responded. Lily and Jesse glanced at each other. False hope was a terrible thing. "I'm sorry," Lily whispered.

"But you are right," he insisted. "Let's start looking."

"For what?"

He waved his smart phone around. "We can look for her." Jesse handed Lily the phone.

Lily stared at the screen. "You had better pull over somewhere and do this yourself."

He nodded and pulled into the next exit. They parked at the truck stop, and Jesse took the phone back. "This may take awhile. We can have a bathroom break and maybe an early lunch if anyone is hungry."

Lily climbed out and opened the car door for Annie. Her sister was pale. Lily gave her sister a long hug, then embraced Mary, who had joined them. Together they moved toward the truck stop building.

"What is he doing?" Mary asked.

"I have no idea," Lily told her. She held open the door.

"Jesse can find her if anyone can," Annie said, "and we have prayed."

Annie took Mary's hand. The two seemed to draw strength from each other, which was how things should be.

There were bathrooms to the right and a food court to the left. Ten minutes later they were seated in one of the booths. Jesse was still out in his car, his head bent over his phone.

Lily wanted to help him, be with him, and share this experience with him. Their time together was limited. She could feel the moments slipping away. Jesse had agreed to help her with the search for Annie's Mamm, but in his heart Jesse did this for Annie. Nothing else explained his dedication and devotion to the task. Jesse's face practically glowed when he came back from those times he had spent alone with Annie. Jesse's face never glowed when he spent time with her.

"He's coming in," Mary whispered, hope alive in her voice.

Jesse entered through the double doors and slid into the booth with them.

"Well?" Lily asked. "Did you find anything?"

Jesse held up his phone. "An address near here. Her name is Alisha, but we don't know what the last name is. They have lived in one location for a long time. Hopefully from near the time Bernice told us Alisha moved to the area."

"And why Fort Wayne?" Annie asked.

"There are large Amish communities near here, to the south as well as farther north. We will continue looking."

Nobody said anything, but everyone knew: This was like looking for a needle in a haystack.

"We had better eat to keep our strength up." Jesse tried to smile. "But we have all day."

Late that day, the sun had sunk below the horizon, and dusk had begun to fall. Jesse pulled into a small convenience store near the town of Nappanee, Indiana. He had another address on his phone, but they were exhausted and ready to settle down for the night. There were motels available in the area, but they needed something more. Did he dare?

"I have a match in this area," he told them. "A goot one, but it's late, and we should go to my cousin's place tonight." Silence greeted him, and Jesse attempted a laugh. "Tired of my wild goose chases?"

"You are giving us the only hope we have," Annie said from the back seat.

He could have kissed the girl, and for more reasons than one. They had spent the entire day knocking on doors and receiving blank looks when they explained their purpose for calling.

"We could get a full meal and a warm bed at the Yoder house." He tried to sound hopeful.

"And impose on your cousin?" The question came from Lily.

"Yah, why not? He's not the same cousin we stayed with on our way to Pennsylvania. Besides, we're all tired, and maybe they would have suggestions. Alisha has to be in the area somewhere."

There were no further protests, and Jesse started the drive through Nappanee. A mile east of town he pulled into a long lane and parked beside the rambling barn. A bearded man appeared in the barn door and approached them.

Jesse climbed out. "Hello, Ezra."

His cousin's face changed from puzzlement to a broad smile. "Well, look what the wind blew in. Jesse Yoder." The two embraced. "What brings you back to Nappanee? I thought your stomping grounds were around Goshen."

"I've moved back to Nebraska," Jesse told him. "Haven't gotten rid of the car yet, but I'm planning to."

"Well, what do you know?" His cousin grinned. "Wild Jesse is settling down. Who would have thought?"

Jesse lowered his voice. "We need a place to stay for the night, the three girls and me."

"Three girls?" Ezra laughed. "You're not running from the law, are you?"

Jesse laughed. "No, just Bishop Mast from Lancaster."

His cousin chuckled. "Never heard of the man. Mind filling me in before I decide?"

Jesse filled him in.

"Quite a tale," his cousin said when Jesse was done. "But it seems like you have the proof with you." He peered at the car where the three worried faces looked back at him. "And I might know an Alisha. She's English. Married, I think. Works at the tourist center, in fact. She's a decent woman from what I can tell."

"You know where she lives?"

"I suppose we could find out, but it's a little late now."

"So you'll put us up for the night?"

"And feed you." His cousin's grin was back. "With three girls' help with supper, I doubt Wauneta will object."

Jesse pounded his cousin on the back and led him to the car for introductions.

19

With the glow of dawn on the horizon outside the window, Annie exited from the Yoders' upstairs bedroom where the girls had spent the night. Jesse had slept on the couch and would be up already. She had heard footsteps stirring downstairs an hour ago before she dozed off again. They had been tired last night. No, more like exhausted to the bone. How long could this search continue? Its toll on body and spirit was intense.

She was grateful for the help she had received thus far though. That Bishop Mast had not yet contacted this community in his search for his daughter meant that no one in Nebraska had given him much information. Otherwise Jesse's old haunts would have been the next places the bishop called from his phone shack. He would want to close as many doors to them as possible.

Annie tiptoed down the stairs and pushed open the door at the bottom. The soft glow of the kerosene lamp from the kitchen doorway flowed into the darkened living room. Annie tiptoed around the corner.

Wauneta Yoder glanced up from the kitchen stove. "Goot morning, Annie. You didn't have to get up."

"Yah, I did," Annie protested. "You have a house full of Kinner, and you're making breakfast for us."

Wauneta's smile filled her face. "A few more eggs, a few more slices of bacon, and extra oatmeal in the pot. It's not a problem."

"Let me help." Annie stepped closer to the stove.

Wauneta nodded. "You can watch the bacon. Jesse is out in the barn with Ezra."

"I thought so." Annie ducked her head as heat rose into her face. Why was she blushing this morning?

"Jesse seems quite devoted to the task of finding your Mamm."

"Yah, I know. We couldn't have come this far without him." Annie checked the bacon frying in the pan.

Wauneta's smile was gone. "Not to burst your bubble, but you do know about Jesse's past, don't you?"

Annie pulled in her breath. "Yah, he told me. About the accident, and Yolanda."

"I see," Wauneta mused. "I thought he was sweet on you."

Annie looked away. "I don't know about that. We have become friends. I'm on a search for my Mamm, and Jesse is on his way back to the community."

"You're not thinking of jumping the fence, are you?" Horror filled Wauneta's voice.

"No, but I don't know what I will find. What if my Mamm wants or needs us to stay with her? I have so many unanswered questions."

"Is it true that Mary is Bishop Mast's daughter from Lancaster County?"

"Do you know him?"

Wauneta shook her head. "Not personally, but if he's a bishop and you have his daughter against his will, then the girl should go back."

Annie tried to breathe evenly. "If there was a problem with putting us up for the night, you should have told Jesse as much. We could have gone to a motel."

Wauneta attempted a smile. "Ezra wouldn't have turned his cousin away regardless of what I would have said."

"I am sorry about this. We will leave now." Annie stepped back from the stove.

"Oh no." The horror was back on Wauneta's face. "I didn't mean that. I am the one who is sorry. You are very welcome here. I just wanted to get some things straight and make sure you knew what you were getting into with Jesse. He led quite the wild life in this area."

"Others do the same on their Rumspringa." Annie turned the bacon.

"That still doesn't make it right, and with Jesse there was the accident. Maybe that's what woke him up."

An awkward silence gripped the kitchen. What was she to say? Clearly Wauneta did not share her husband's welcome of this party of Amish vagabonds. Behind them the stairs squeaked, and both Mary and Lily appeared.

Wauneta's smile was back, as if nothing uncomfortable had been said. "Goot morning. You are up bright and early."

Both of them returned the greeting.

"Let me help with something," Mary offered.

"Are you all right?" Lily whispered in Annie's ear.

Annie pressed back the quick tears. Someone had noticed. For once she regretted that Lily knew her so well. "Can you cover for me?"

Lily nodded with a worried look on her face.

"I'm going to the barn to see if the men need any help," Annie told them. "I think things are taken care of here."

She slipped through the washroom before anyone could protest. Not that they would have. There was nothing wrong with helping the men in the barn. What was wrong was that this search for her Mamm had dragged trouble behind them like a sack of rotting potatoes. How could such a pure desire in her heart have led to such disruption in people's lives?

Annie burst through the barn door and paused to catch her breath. A disheveled appearance would only provoke questions from the men. A soft glow of lantern light shone in the distance. Annie made her way deeper into the barn. She saw Jesse's back first. He leaned against the cow stanchion, deep in conversation with his cousin. The low murmur of their voices rose above the soft mooing of the cows.

"She's got a right to find her Mamm," Jesse was saying.

"You sure you're not doing this because of some future plans, like—" Ezra's voice was drowned out by a cow's bellow.

Was there no escape from disapproval this morning? Hadn't Ezra welcomed them into his home last night? Had Wauneta's fears taken root in Ezra's heart? From what she had been told in the kitchen, Annie guessed that Wauneta had given her husband an earful after the party had retired.

"Annie!" Jesse exclaimed and waved his hand. "Goot morning."

Annie forced a smile. "Four women is one too many in the kitchen. Can I help out here?"

"Ah!" Ezra's face glowed with the same smile he had given them last night. "I see I have all kinds of help this morning. Mind helping Jesse feed the horses?"

"It would be my pleasure."

"Just point the way," Jesse added.

Ezra motioned toward the back of the barn. "Hay is in the loft. You know your way around."

"I haven't been out here that often." Jesse gave Ezra a wink. "Come." He took Annie's hand and led the way.

"You're making a scene," she whispered. "I heard him expressing doubt about us."

Jesse chuckled. "Then we are 'us.'"

"Please don't tease me this morning, Jesse. I can't take it right now. Wauneta already chewed my ears off in the kitchen."

"So that's why you're out here."

"Yah. And four women really are too many in a kitchen."

"I'm sure Wauneta isn't too serious, just worried. Amish people are that way. I did things I shouldn't have. I'm supposing she made sure you knew that."

Annie regarded him for a moment. "You knew she would, and yet you brought us here."

"Hey." Jesse opened the feed bin. "We needed a full Amish meal and Amish hospitality to comfort our souls and rest our bodies. I have nothing to hide. I don't want my past to stay hidden. Did she tell you anything I haven't?"

"No." Annie took the bucket of feed from him. "Half for each horse?"

"Something like that." He was clearly distracted. "I hope we find your Mamm this morning, Annie. I was comparing more notes with Ezra about the last address I found last night, and his descriptions of this woman hold much promise."

The tears stung again. "You know we can't go on much longer. I have caused too many problems. I might have ruined Mary's life. And I've taken up so much of your time. We have to go back. I must give up this foolish dream."

He pried her fingers from the bucket handle. "I want nothing more than to find your Mamm, and we're not giving up until we do."

"You know there are limits."

"Not for you."

The tears trickled now. "You know I'm not the right woman for you. I don't bring goot things into your life. Not like Lily would."

He shushed her with a touch of his finger on her lips. "Don't say that. We are finding your Mamm, and then you are coming back to the community with us."

"Jesse." Her eyes begged. "You and I . . . Ezra and Wauneta are right about us, along with everyone in the community back in Nebraska, I'm sure. We don't belong together."

"Do you really mean that?" He studied her intently.

Annie looked away.

"Answer me!" He stepped closer. "Does your heart really say that?"

Annie pressed her hand against her chest to still the rapid pounding.

"I know it doesn't," he said quietly, "and neither does mine."

"But how can this ever be?"

He set the bucket of feed on the ground and reached for her. "I don't know, but I love you. With everything in me, I love you. That is what I do know."

With a sob, she flew into his arms and clung to him until the sharp neigh of horses pulled them apart.

Annie smoothed her apron with both hands and straightened her Kapp. "I'm sorry about that. I had no right to take advantage of your kindness."

He lifted her gaze with his fingers under her chin and silenced her with a deep, abiding kiss.

Back in the kitchen, Lily laid out the utensils on the table. The bacon warmed in the oven, and Mary flipped the last of the eggs in the pan. Wauneta had been chattering away ever since Annie had made her quick exit from the kitchen. What had passed between the two women? Lily hadn't dared ask—yet.

"Our oldest will be in school next year," Wauneta was saying. "How they grow up so quickly only the Lord knows. Not yesterday it seems I gave birth to the child, and wondered where the grace would come from to raise him into a God-fearing young man. Now we have five, and the youngest is in diapers. The Lord has blessed us."

"What did you and Annie talk about before we came down?" Lily asked, interrupting her.

Wauneta's voice ceased in midsentence. "This and that. Why?"

"What did you tell her?" Lily faced the woman. "Annie is my sister. I have a right to know."

"Well, I suppose so." Wauneta's glance passed between Lily and Mary.

"She can hear it too," Lily said. "Mary is Annie's twin and is family."

"Yah, I guess," Wauneta said, but doubt flickered on her face. "It's just some things are not for everyone's ears."

Lily tilted her head and waited.

"Okay, I'll speak." Wauneta shrugged. "Jesse lived quite the wild life while on his Rumspringa in this area. I thought Annie should know."

"What has that got to do with us being here?"

Wauneta snorted. "You are not blind, girl, surely. Those two are quite sweet on each other."

Lily winced.

Wauneta clucked her tongue. "I guess you are the one I should have been telling it to. Obviously you don't know."

"So Annie knew?"

"That Jesse was driving with his English girlfriend, Yolanda, when she was killed? Annie claimed Jesse told her."

Mary let out a little yelp and collapsed on a kitchen chair.

"At least someone has an appropriate reaction," Wauneta said. "I was beginning to wonder."

Lily's head spun and she clutched the edge of the kitchen table. Jesse had shared this with Annie but not her. But had she wanted to know? She had told Jesse that nothing mattered.

"What exactly happened?" Lily croaked.

"Depends on whose version you believe," Wauneta said. "There was a large dog in the road, yah, and the police say Jesse wasn't drinking—or worse—but I know what wild young people do on Rumspringa."

"How was it that Yolanda died and Jesse didn't?"

"They hit a tree, and the impact was on Yolanda's side. Neither of them was wearing a seat belt, which in this case probably saved his life. Jesse was thrown from the car. The police found him unconscious from a concussion, but beyond a few scratches and bruises, that was it."

Lily opened her mouth but closed it again when the washroom door opened and Annie came through with Jesse and Ezra right behind her.

"Breakfast ready yet?" Ezra boomed.

Jesse glanced around the kitchen. Breakfast was ready, but the Yoder children were still not up. From the troubled look on Lily's face and the dash Wauneta made for the stairs, the conversation between the women had hit rough waters. Mary was seated on a kitchen chair and looked ready to faint.

"Well!" Ezra stroked the last of the water from his beard. "Looks like the children aren't here, but Wauneta will have them ready in a moment. Everyone be seated. We can wait a few more minutes."

"I'll go help her," Lily said and hurried off.

Mary appeared to gather her strength and followed Lily at a slower speed.

Ezra peered around. "Anyone mind explaining to me what is going on here? There was plenty of help this morning, and Wauneta still doesn't have the children up."

"She was probably telling the others what she told me," Annie ventured.

Ezra attempted a laugh. "At least breakfast is ready."

"We didn't mean to disturb your house." Jesse gave Ezra an apologetic look. "I figured Wauneta might object, but not this much. I'm sorry."

Ezra sobered. "Yah, Wauneta was pretty upset last night, but I told her you would straighten things out. Not that the woman was convinced, and I do understand her point."

Jesse nodded. "I didn't hide anything from Annie, and we needed a place to stay for the night."

"You don't have to apologize," Ezra interrupted him. "It's okay. I'm on your side. The past is the past, and we all have done things we shouldn't."

"I did some pretty awful things." Jesse met Ezra's gaze.

Ezra shook his head. "What is important right now is that you find this woman who is the girls' Mamm. I have a feeling a lot will settle down once you finish this journey."

"You think so?"

"I know so," Ezra assured him. "You are certainly doing the Lord's work if trouble is coming after you like this."

Annie sat down beside Jesse, and her hand slipped into his. He didn't dare look at her. He had held Annie in his arms only moments before and kissed her, but the gulf was still vast between them. If today was another failure, their chances of bridging the distance would worsen. He didn't dare think about that.

Annie was right. Her search couldn't go on much longer. Even with success, he couldn't make Annie remain in the community, and he couldn't return to the English world with her if Annie decided to leave.

Ezra elbowed him. "Cheer up, cousin. I will pray for you. You will feel better after the wunderbah breakfast these women have cooked up."

Jesse tried to smile as Wauneta bustled back into the kitchen with her children behind her. Lily followed with a grim look, and Mary was still white-faced. Jesse doubted if breakfast would repair the shock in Lily's heart. He should have told her, even when she had claimed that nothing would matter. Only Annie had drawn the deep secrets from his heart. He squeezed her hand, and Annie's fingers moved in response.

"Let us give thanks for this food," Ezra said, and they bowed their heads in prayer.

20

The drive to the new address went quickly. They bypassed the tourist sites outside of Nappanee and ended up in front of a small blue bungalow set half a mile from the highway. *Is this finally the end of our journey?* Annie held Mary's hand in the back seat and begged heaven for a positive answer.

She found her voice. "We will go first this time."

Neither Lily nor Jesse objected as Annie climbed out and waited for Mary to join her. In slow motion they approached the front door, and Annie knocked.

An English woman answered the door with a puzzled look on her face. "Yes? Can I help you?"

The words stuck in Annie's mouth.

"Are you Alisha Westby?" Mary asked from beside her.

"Yes." The confusion remained on the woman's face.

"Was your maiden name Mandarin?" Mary was still asking the questions. Where did her twin find the strength to speak at a moment like this?

"Yes." Bafflement turned to wonder. Alisha shook her head as if to clear her eyes. "Sorry. I thought you looked familiar for a moment. Are you twins?"

They nodded together.

"Are you adopted?"

They nodded again.

Alisha had grown pale. "Is this what I think it is? How did you find me?"

"Are we welcome?" Mary asked.

A man appeared behind Alisha.

"Good morning." He gave them a smile.

"This is Annie and Mary." Alisha's voice was faint.

"Did you meet Alisha at work?" His smile grew. "She makes all kinds of friends with the Amish."

Alisha's mouth worked soundlessly.

"Are . . . are we welcome?" Annie asked this time.

Alisha's legs seemed to give way.

Her husband caught her. "Alisha! What is this about?"

"Take me to the couch, Bob. I need to sit down."

"And these girls?" Bob glanced at them.

In answer, Alisha reached for the twins and leaned on them while she led the way into the house. Bob muttered something Annie couldn't hear. He brought up the rear. There was no sign of Lily or Jesse. They must have decided to stay in the car. She wanted Jesse with her, but perhaps his absence was for the best. Jesse would want to know that he had not influenced her in any way as she met her real Mamm for the first time and looked the future in the eyes.

Alisha motioned for them to sit on the couch. "Get me a chair, Bob. I can stand for a moment alone."

Bob looked ready to say something but moved off instead. He returned with a chair and helped Alisha ease into it.

They looked at each other silently for a long time.

"What is this about?" Bob finally asked.

Tears formed on Alisha's cheeks. "I think these are my lost babies, Bob, but maybe we should start at the beginning. Can you tell me, girls, about the woman you are looking for?"

Annie hurried through the details—their arrival in Lancaster County, their visit to the midwife Olivia Raber, the papers Lily had obtained from the Hope Clinic, and their discovery of each other. Long before she finished, the tears had turned into a flood from Alisha's eyes.

"You are our Mamm, are you not?" Annie choked.

Mary clung to her arm, her fingers digging deeply.

"I am," Alisha said simply. "And you have found me. I tried not to leave a trail. I didn't want to interfere with your lives."

"You thought we wouldn't search for you?"

"What mother leaves her babies like I did? Not a good mother. Why would you want to find me?"

"But we did!" the girls exclaimed together.

"Since the day I was told that I was adopted, I have wanted to know who my birth Mamm is," Annie added. "You can't imagine how badly I have wanted to know."

Mary nodded and added, "I did secretly, but I didn't dare speak up like Annie did."

Alisha had grown pale. "You were separated?"

Neither girl responded, but pain filled Alisha's face.

"I thought I knew the worst!" she cried. "What did I do?" She buried her face in her hands.

Both girls rose as one and moved Alisha to sit between them on the couch.

Annie stroked Alisha's arm. "It was probably very hard to find a home for twin girls. But we have found each other and you, Mamm. That's all that matters now. This will be the healing of all our hearts, and the sharing of our joy together."

Alisha wiped her eyes to stem the gush of tears.

"We love you, Mamm," Mary whispered, as if testing the word. "It's okay. We understand why you did what you did. We know you love us."

Alisha took Mary in her arms, and the two clung to each other.

"Tell me about your lives." Alisha let go enough to gather Annie close.

Bob had vanished into the kitchen. This was their moment, the end of the journey, but yet a new beginning that formed among the three of them with each soft tick of the clock set up against the living room wall. Annie smiled, noticing for the first time that Alisha had an Amish-made grandfather clock.

Mary noticed too, from the look on her face. "There's not much to say about my life," she said. "I'm an Amish girl, the only child in a bishop's household."

Alisha's eyes shone. "A bishop. You are an Amish bishop's daughter."

Mary nodded. "My adoptive parents love me, and I'm engaged to a goot man."

"An Amish man?"

Mary smiled. "Yah. I wouldn't marry anyone else. I am happy to be Amish."

Alisha took both of Mary's hands in hers. "Oh, child, I cannot tell you how happy that makes me. I had hoped, dreamed, and dared to pray that you would both find the peace and fulfillment in life that I never had. The Lord has been gracious to me in these later years with Bob, but it was not always so. When I became pregnant with you, I had no support from my parents. I wanted you to be raised where parents loved their children. The Amish I knew from Lancaster County had families filled with love and support. That's what I wanted for my girls. I hope you understand."

Both girls nodded.

"I only asked that you be given to Amish parents." The tears were back. "I never thought they would separate you. Did you know you were twins?"

"Maybe in our hearts," Annie allowed. "But we didn't know for sure until my sister got the paperwork that proved it."

"I hope you can forgive me." Alisha held their hands tightly. "For everything. For giving you away and letting you be separated. For having caused such pain. For not being the mother I should have been."

"You did what you could," Annie said, comforting her. "And look at who we are. We have not suffered from what you did."

Alisha gulped. "You are so kind, so gentle, so like the people I have loved and could never be like. The Lord has given me the desire of my heart. You have found me. My girls—my babies—are such beautiful young women now. You glow with health and happiness. I could never have done this for you, brought up to be such gorgeous and tender women. And you are loved at home. I know you are. I can see it in your faces. Much more than I could have ever loved you, with my problems."

"Mamm, don't say that," Annie protested. "You did what you could, and the Lord blessed. Now we have found you, and we can always be together. Well, almost. At least you can come to Mary's wedding this fall, and to mine when I marry."

"You have no beloved one?" Alisha was incredulous.

"She does," Mary said, her voice teasing. "A very handsome and dashing man."

"Oh!" Alisha glowed. "I wish to see both of them soon. If it is allowed."

"Mary exaggerates a little," Annie said. "But I do care about—"

"You are in love with him," Mary said with a giggle. "Madly."

"What sweet quarreling you two do," Alisha gushed. "I am so happy, so deliriously happy. Just give me a moment. I have to call in and cancel work. We have to spend the whole day together. Can you do that? And stay the night. I can't let you out of my sight just yet—maybe never."

Alisha made a dash for the kitchen, and Bob stuck his head into the room. "Howdy, girls," he said. "You have made your mother very happy. I hope you know that. She has grieved since I first met her, but she has always refused to search for you. She said it wasn't decent."

"I wish she would have," Annie told him.

Bob smiled. "She wanted the best for you. That's why she didn't. She has always loved you with her whole heart."

"We know that," Annie said happily, and Mary nodded beside her.

Outside the house, Lily shifted in the car, her gaze fixed on the door of the small blue bungalow. "Do you think we should go inside?"

"We'd better give them all the time they need," Jesse cautioned. "But it seems we have finally found their Mamm."

"We have," Lily agreed. She glanced at him. "And I was right."

Jesse laughed. "You usually are."

"Don't tease me," she chided. "I'm serious. You have your Amish girl now. One you can love."

"I'm sorry about this." Jesse didn't look at Lily. "And I'm sorry for what Wauneta told you this morning. I should have been more forthright."

"You told Annie." Lily couldn't keep the edge out of her voice.

"Are you and I ever going to make our peace?"

"Could we, if I am wrong about Annie's Mamm?"

"But you are never wrong. Remember?"

Lily laughed. "I am often wrong. Look how wrong I have been with my feelings for you."

Jesse sobered. "Would you really settle for a man who killed his girlfriend in a car wreck?"

"You didn't kill her, and I don't care what you did. I already told you that."

"There is something wrong about that attitude. You know that."

Lily sighed. "I suppose so. I'm irrational when it comes to you."

"My past would bother you later—I know it would. You are what Annie isn't."

Lily winced. "I wish that wasn't true."

"But it is. We can't change what we are."

"Then why have I wanted to? For years now I have loved you and been willing to become whatever it took to make you love me."

"I'm not a psychologist, Lily. I'm just an ordinary guy who went home hoping to leave his past behind him."

Lily sat upright. "And you would have. You would have accepted me, taken a chance with us, if—"

"If we hadn't come on this search," he finished.

"Yah. And would you have ever told me about Yolanda?"

"Would you have wanted to know?"

Lily shook her head.

"There's your answer. Do you think that would have been wise?"

"I thought you weren't a psychologist."

Jesse grinned. "I'm not."

Lily turned her head as the front door of the house opened and Annie and Mary hurried toward the car.

Jesse waited until Lily had climbed out to speak with Annie and Mary before he got out of the car and approached the three girls.

"She is our Mamm," Annie gushed, her face aglow. "Somehow I knew the moment we walked up on her front porch."

Mary said nothing, but her sparkling eyes spoke volumes.

"So where do we go from here?" Lily asked.

"We're spending the day and the night at least with our Mamm,"

Annie said. "We need our suitcases. Maybe you can check in with us tomorrow and see how we are doing. I hope that's not imposing too much, but we have to spend some time together now that we've found each other."

Jesse moved closer, but Annie appeared to be caught up in her joy, transported to another world. He wanted to open his arms and draw her close, but she chattered away as if he didn't exist.

"Come inside and meet Alisha." Annie grabbed the suitcases out of the trunk of the car.

Lily and Jesse followed the twins inside.

Alisha was seated on the couch, and they shook hands. The woman's face was filled with happiness, but she only had eyes for her two daughters.

"We should be going," Lily said, almost at once.

Annie followed them to the front door. "Is this okay?" She looked at Jesse for the first time. "You two will be on your own for a while."

"It's okay." Jesse forced a smile. "I'm glad we've finally come to the end of our journey. Take your time, and call me tomorrow on my cell when you are ready." He pulled a card from his pocket.

"Thank you, Jesse." Annie came closer to take the piece of paper. "Thank you so much. This would never have happened without you and Lily."

Annie's fingers touched his and lingered there for a second before she was gone, hurrying back to her Mamm's side.

"Maybe I was wrong about Annie's devotion to you," Lily muttered at the end of the sidewalk.

"Which would be the most unusual thing," Jesse reminded her as they climbed into the car. He had no agreement with Annie, just the memory of her sweet kisses planted firmly in his mind. But before this, with Yolanda, he had dared dream of a life spent with someone who stirred his heart deeply. He had also vowed he would never position himself to feel such pain again.

Jesse started the car and turned around in the driveway. He glanced over at Lily, who was staring back at the blue bungalow. What was his problem that he couldn't love the woman who loved him with the greatest dedication, for the greatest length of time, for reasons he couldn't fathom?

Lily said nothing as they bounced out of the driveway and roared east toward Nappanee. The whole day stretched in front of them, empty and void without Annie. Was this what the end of rainbows contained?

"What shall we do?" he ventured.

"We're together." She smiled. "Just you and me. Finally!"

"You want to be a tourist for the day?"

Lily turned up her nose. "I'm Amish. Why would I want to see how the Amish live?"

"We could pay for a buggy ride," he teased.

Lily rolled her eyes. "Let's look for a quilt shop."

"You want to go to a quilt shop?"

"You would take Annie there, even if you didn't want to go."

He looked away. "Annie's not here."

"But I am."

He forced a smile. "Then I will take you to a quilt shop. There's Martin's right out on County Road 46."

"Sounds wunderbah to me." But Lily wasn't smiling. "You know, we could have been great together, Jesse."

The girl didn't give up. "Just for the record, I don't object to quilt shops."

A hint of a smile played on Lily's face.

21

The lunch hour passed with quick sandwiches prepared and eaten in the kitchen. Bob shooed them out into the living room again.

"I'll clean up what little there is," he insisted with a smile.

They talked while he did so, the twins clustered on either side of their Mamm on the couch.

"You were such little sweethearts," Alisha said, her hands in theirs. "I begged for a glimpse after the birth, and the nurse relented though she wasn't supposed to. I almost wavered in my resolve, seeing your tiny faces, your little arms waving about. That's why they don't let you see your babies before they are taken away." Alisha paused to compose herself. "The nurse hurried me out of the nursery, but the memory of you was already in my heart. I was given that much of a gift, and I comforted myself that you were in good hands. I did follow up with the Hope Clinic later, and they assured me that you had been given to Amish parents like I requested. Maybe they didn't know about the separation, but that doesn't matter now. You made it back to me." Alisha beamed at them through her tears. "I've lived close to Amish communities all my life, trying to imagine what it was like for my precious girls. You must have been treated so well and raised with such love and kindness. That was something I never knew."

"We were," Annie assured her. "I have nothing but fond memories of growing up. Mamm and Daett were very open with me about my adoption and loved me even when I wanted to search for you."

"Did they oppose you?" Alisha asked in alarm.

Annie forced a smile. "Not really, but they had their doubts. They saw dangers, and the truth was I didn't know what I would find at the end of my journey."

Understanding flickered on Alisha's face. "I can see that—the woman who gave away her babies."

"No," the girls said together.

"It wasn't about you as a mother," Annie said. "They feared the English world. They thought maybe we would want to join you, that you would encourage us to join you."

Tears again trickled down Alisha's face. "And yet you came, right through your fears."

"We loved you," they said in unison again.

"I had to find you," Mary added. "Whatever the cost. I would regret knowing I had the chance to meet you and was overcome by my fears."

Alisha wiped her eyes. "I know enough about your culture to understand, but let me assure you that I have nothing like that in mind for either of you. In fact, I want nothing more than for each of you to find Amish husbands and lead the life I never had. Only in my later years have I found peace with Bob. You will never experience the pain I traveled through."

"Though I can be a pain sometimes too!" Bob shouted from the kitchen.

A smile flickered on Alisha's face. "The man is such a dear. If I had met him earlier, perhaps things would have been different. We were never able to have children, but I have you now." Alisha's fingers squeezed Annie's hand.

"And we have you," Mary whispered. "Everything I have gone

through was worth the cost. Daett might even give his approval now."

Annie stopped Mary with a quick shake of her head. Too much information was not wise.

Mary seemed to understand and gave Alisha a hug.

"My little sweet baby." Alisha stroked Mary's face. "Only you are not so little anymore. All grown up and soon to be married. Will I get a wedding invitation?"

"Of course! We will have you seated in the front row in a place of honor. You won't be able to understand a word, or at least very few. The sermons and the vows will be in German. We can't change that."

"I wouldn't want you to." Alisha had drawn Mary close. "Just being there is enough. To see my little girl married and settled down. What a beautiful woman you are. The Lord must have heard the cry of my heart. He knows I didn't pay much attention to Him most of the time, but He still paid attention to me. I didn't even believe this day would happen."

"But here we are," Annie said.

"And what about you?" Alisha faced Annie with tearstained cheeks. "When is your wedding?"

Heat flushed into Annie's face.

"That's a good answer," Alisha chuckled.

"We . . . ," Annie managed. "We aren't even dating."

"Annie is very much in love, and so is Jesse," Mary spoke up. "I can tell. Their hearts are knit close."

Annie stilled the protest that rose to her lips. *If only this were true.*

"And you will let me know when you have little ones. Both of you," Alisha continued.

Now the heat flamed. Annie glanced at Mary, whose cheeks

equally glowed.

Alisha appeared not to notice. "I guess that would be allowed, wouldn't it?"

"Oh, yah!" the girls exclaimed together.

"If there are any Kinner," Mary said. "That is up to the Lord's will, of course."

Alisha's eyes twinkled. "I will assume the Lord will decide in my favor, now that He has given me this great gift of seeing you."

The three laughed together.

"You will write and tell me, won't you? Or can you call from the phone shacks?"

"We can." Annie nodded. "And you will come then, won't you, and visit us? I mean, people will know who you are by then, having been to our weddings."

Alisha stared first at one and then the other.

"You must come." Mary took Alisha's hand in both of hers. "We can't take pictures, so you will have to come in person and stay for a week or two. Maybe longer if you can."

Alisha appeared unable to speak for a second. "This is more than I dared hope for and dream about. My girls are Amish and soon to wed, and I get to see the grandchildren."

Bob appeared and placed a box of tissues in front of them. Annie handed one to Alisha. Mary helped herself.

"Can I see an Amish schoolhouse someday?" Alisha finally asked. "I've always wanted to see one, but I never dared ask."

"Yah, of course." Annie clutched a tissue in her hand. "When you visit Nebraska, I will take you down to the schoolhouse I attended."

"I can do the same," Mary said.

"So you mean I can see the very place where you walked in the door on your first day of school?"

Annie managed a laugh. "My desk is still there. Little changes in Amish life."

"I can show you where Ben first noticed me," Mary added. "He was standing at home plate ready to bat, and I was catcher that day. He glanced back to ask me, 'Do you think you can do this?' I gave him a glare. 'Of course,' I said. 'I can throw bales of hay into the horse stalls.'" A smile flickered on Mary's face. "Ben was impressed. My heart skipped a beat for the first time, and I knew he was the one I would love. Well, I expected we would get together after that. Ben took his time; he's cautious. But I waited."

"And how did you meet this Jesse of yours?" Alisha asked Annie.

Annie looked away. "He's not my boyfriend." When she glanced at them, she saw both her Mamm and her twin gazing back at her expectantly. She sighed. Denial was useless. "On this trip, I guess. We grew up in the same community, but he had no interest in me in school, so I have no story like Mary does."

"I'm sure you both have sweet tales to tell." Alisha's smile split her face. "Both of my girls will have Amish husbands. I cannot ask for more, and yet so much more is given me for which I am not worthy."

"Stop knocking yourself," Bob scolded. "You are a special lady."

"See?" Alisha asked, gesturing. "That's what I mean, and now I have you two as well."

They clung to each other until Annie pulled away. "We should prepare supper since we're staying with you tonight."

"Supper!" Alisha exclaimed. "Bob can bring in something. I want to spend all my time with you, with both of you."

Annie stood. "Working in the kitchen is the best way to spend time together. We will not bring in food tonight. That would be wrong. What we need is a big Amish supper to celebrate. Mary and I will have it ready by six or so, and then we can eat. You can be with us the whole time."

Alisha's face glowed. "My two beautiful Amish girls, cooking in my kitchen."

"There—I am right."

The three of them traipsed into the kitchen.

"Do I get to eat this supper?" Bob asked pitifully.

"Only if you behave," Mary said, shaking a finger at him in mock sternness.

Their laughter filled the house.

Meanwhile, Lily left the car and strode purposefully toward the small quilt shop south of Nappanee. Jesse had been true to his word. This was their third stop, and he was managing to pretend to enjoy himself. But why was she doing this? Annie was back at the house with her birth Mamm and with Mary. Decisions would be made that affected everyone, but she shouldn't gather up hopes with such a thin rope. Jesse's face darkened in those moments when he thought he was alone, like at the last stop when she had snuck up on him in the back aisle stacked high with cloth bolts.

"Thinking of buying for a shirt?" she had teased.

Jesse had given her a clearly forced smile. "A blue one would be nice," he said. "Maybe a Sunday shirt for when we get back to the community."

"So you are coming back?"

He hadn't answered, because that wasn't the question. They both knew what burned in their hearts. Would Annie come back after she had met with her Mamm? Could she be content—happy—again in the Amish way of life?

Lily kept a pace ahead of Jesse as they passed the painted sign, *Country Quilt Creations*, with a pretty quilt drawn above the words. This was an English-run place. No Amish person would place such a fancy sign outside, even if it drew in customers. That was not the Amish way. Annie's sign back home in Nebraska was written simply on a white background. Lily reached for the doorknob automatically, her mind elsewhere. Her garden would have grown high by now. Mamm would struggle to find the time for its proper care. She should not have come along on this trip. Annie could have managed on her own. Lily pushed the bitter thought away and held the door wide for Jesse.

He smiled his thanks. "Nice place."

"Yah, it is," Lily agreed.

A full-size quilt was set up in the front room. It displayed a brown-and-white hexagon pattern with interlocking green links, done without excessive busyness. Someone knew what they were doing with quilt design.

"What can I do for you?" a lady with a pleasant face inquired.

"Just looking," Jesse told her, "but thank you."

"Let me know if I can help," the lady said and retreated.

What is an Amish girl doing in an English quilt shop? That was the unspoken question that hung in the air. Jesse still looked English and had experienced the ways of the English on his Rumspringa. Lily was a simple girl. She had always been that way, yet Jesse might still decide that she was the right choice as a Frau for him. The hope simply wouldn't die.

Lily forced herself to breathe evenly and admire the quilt at length.

"Plain and beautiful," Jesse observed.

She gave him a warm smile. On that at least they agreed.

He winked and led the way farther into the shop. There was a small red-and-white poinsettia quilt with green leaves set up on a table. *Quilting classes*, the sign nearby read; *$25 sign-up fee*.

"Want to apply?" Jesse teased.

"I already know how."

"I know you do," he said, serious now. "You have a lot of wunderbah abilities and talents."

Just none that could make you love me, she almost retorted. Instead she said, "I wonder how my garden looks back home."

"We should be back soon," he said.

Lily nodded and walked deeper into the small shop. Again, that was not the real question.

Later that evening, when they had finished supper and cleanup at Ezra and Wauneta's home, Jesse stepped up to the kitchen doorway. "Do you want to go outside for a moment? We can sit on the front porch swing."

"I guess so." Lily twisted the washcloth in her hand. "Just a moment and I'll be out."

The poor girl. Jesse left the doorway and gave his cousin a grin on the way past him. Ezra raised his eyebrows, but didn't say anything. His cousin was up-to-date on the day's occurrences: the meeting of the twins' Mamm and the decision by Annie and Mary to stay the night. But the aimless tour of the county's quilt shops had been touched on only in passing. The struggle of their hearts remained hidden. Jesse knew what Ezra suspected. Why else would he want to sit alone with Lily on the front porch swing?

Jesse exited the house, leaving the door ajar. Lily's footsteps followed behind him. She was usually the one who faced things, while he avoided conflict. For once he must be honest with her.

He sat down to the squeak of the chains above him. Lily seated herself, but didn't look at him.

"We should talk," he finally said.

"About what?"

"Us. You know what I mean."

She glanced at him. "We've been together most of the day."

"We must decide," he said. "Tonight. Before we know what Annie's decision is. That's the only way to settle this properly."

Lily sighed. "You take me quilt shopping, and we end up on the front porch swing, but this is not what it seems. Am I correct?"

"You need to be honest, Lily. Do you really want the life I can offer? I am what I am. I'm not going to change."

"You think Annie wants this?" Her hand flew into the air. "Whatever you are."

"That doesn't matter. What matters is *us*. What we had once, or what we didn't have. That came first. We should settle *us*."

"And how should we?"

"I don't know. I was tempted this afternoon to propose to you. You have been dedicated to me, to my memory while I was gone, and now that I am back, you say nothing matters that I have done, yet—"

"And yet you don't think that's goot enough."

He regarded her for a long time. "You like straight rows. You like plants that grow as they are supposed to. You like order, the sun rising and setting on time. You like your garden, Lily, and I am not a garden."

"You are a wild garden that needs tending."

He sighed. "I don't want tending. I want love. There is a difference."

"But I do love you!"

"That's what I've always thought—"

"And you doubt me now?"

He shook his head. "Not really."

"Then what, Jesse?"

"It's hard to explain."

"You want more, is that it?"

"I've always wanted more."

"And you always will," she finished for him. Her voice cracked, as he imagined her heart was doing.

He winced. "I suppose so, but that is wrong of me to say, as if there is something not right about you, when you are all that is goot and right in the world. I don't mean to be cruel."

A tear trickled down her cheek. "You speak the truth, Jesse. In the end I don't want a husband who is a garden that always needs tending. There will be other gardens to tend, Kinner perhaps, a future to guard. I would be happier with a man I could trust, not just love. In the end, love that does not include trust is faulty. It is missing something."

He reached for her hand. "You are too goot for me, Lily. That is the real problem."

She pulled her hand away. "No, Jesse. The problem is that you are right for Annie. That is said better. Annie and I have no quarrel about this."

"Let's leave Annie out of this."

Her voice was quiet. "We have, Jesse, and it still doesn't help. I believe you now."

"You believe what? That we can't be?"

"I know that I would regret marrying a man whose heart wasn't fully mine. Regardless of how I felt about him."

His hand slipped from hers and they sat in the falling dusk, the chains of the porch swing squeaking above them.

22

The early-morning colors were still in the sky when Annie stepped out on the front porch of the small bungalow, suitcase in hand. Mary was close behind, followed by Alisha and Bob. They had called Jesse's cell phone late last night, and his Malibu would pull into the lane any time now.

Annie set the suitcase on the floor to give her Mamm a long hug. "Thank you so much for everything you did for us, for meeting with us, for being happy to see us, for being our Mamm."

Alisha clung to Annie, a sob choking in her voice. "You are thanking me? I should be thanking you. You have put right what I did wrong." Alisha held Annie at arm's length. "My beautiful daughter, my baby." Alisha reached for Mary too and pulled both girls close.

"Your ride is here," Bob said. "You will see each other again soon."

"That doesn't make this any easier," Alisha told him.

"You will come visit me first," Mary told her. "Once I'm settled in again, but before the wedding preparations are in full rush."

"I certainly will," Alisha assured her. "I know my way around Lancaster County. Now Nebraska—that is another world."

"Whenever you come is fine." Annie gave her Mamm another embrace. "We have to go or we'll never get off this porch."

"I want to meet this young man again, now that I can actually focus on him," Alisha said as the Malibu came to a stop.

Annie waited while Jesse climbed out and approached the house with Lily right beside him. Annie searched Jesse's face. She didn't want to assume, but they had not spoken yet. Had Jesse made a decision to accept Lily's affections? She couldn't blame him if he had.

Annie put on a brave smile. "Goot morning," she greeted them. "My Mamm would like to meet you again."

Which was partly true. Alisha wanted to meet Jesse, but Lily had played a big part in this search, and she should not be slighted.

Alisha reached for Jesse with both hands, and he didn't object to the hug.

"How are you?" Annie asked Lily, while the two were occupied.

"I had a goot night's sleep at Ezra and Wauneta's place," Lily said, her voice too bright.

More had happened than that from the look on her sister's face. Annie nudged her.

"Jesse and I have come to the end of the road," Lily offered with a weak smile.

Annie tried to breathe. So Jesse and Lily had arrived at an agreement yesterday. Annie's knees shook, but she managed to smile and hug Alisha again before she took her suitcase to the Malibu. Mary had deposited her luggage in the trunk and now ran past Annie to take her final leave of their Mamm.

Annie climbed into the back of the Malibu and waited.

Lily opened the back door. "You should ride in the front, Annie."

"Why?"

"It's decided. It's up to you from here on out."

Annie shook her head. "I'm riding with Mary. That's proper."

Lily gave in. "Okay. But not from Lancaster back to Nebraska. You are riding in the front. Your place is beside Jesse."

Annie stilled her protest. That was what she wanted. Desperately. She had found her Mamm, and now the door was open to Jesse's heart.

Annie pushed open the car door as Mary came down the sidewalk with Jesse behind her. Jesse gave her a tender smile before he walked around the car and climbed in.

"Ready?" Jesse asked over his shoulder.

"Yes!" the twins said as one.

Annie's spirits soared. How wonderful of Lily to let her know before she lingered long in the agony of doubt. She would have tried to accept it if Lily and Jesse had decided otherwise, but at the same time, they never would have. They couldn't have. Annie waved as they drove out of the driveway.

Tears streamed down Mary's face. "We found her, Annie. I still can't believe it."

"Believe it!" Lily said. "Our search is at an end. Now for the return home."

Mary gasped. "Home. Daett." She trembled. "I had almost forgotten about Daett."

"He'll be so happy to see you," Annie told her.

Mary tried to smile, but neither of them was convinced.

"I'll take care of your Daett," Lily said. "I'll go in once we arrive and speak with him."

"*You* will speak with him?" A slight smile played on Jesse's face.

"I will!" Lily declared. "We will finish this journey properly and in goot order. There will be peace for everyone and no more trouble."

"If you say so," Jesse replied.

"I guess you were the one who got the search out of several tight spots," Mary ventured.

"Your Daett will see the light of day once I'm done with him." Lily lifted her nose in the air.

They all laughed. Lily exaggerated, but there was some truth to what she said. Lily was the one who could approach Bishop Mast with courage. She could speak his language if anyone could—faithful, steady, dependable Lily.

"I do think he will!" Jesse declared, as he drove back through Nappanee. "You have the courage, and the record."

"Each to their own God-given gift. That's what I say."

Annie cleared her throat. "Maybe if we share with you what Alisha told us, why she gave her twin babies to the Amish, and how she has lived around Amish communities ever since . . ." The details of the story spilled out with Mary's help. "I think this might help."

"It will," Lily agreed.

Jesse slowed the car for his cousin's driveway. "I think we should stop in to officially say goodbye."

The girls agreed and Jesse parked beside the barn. Ezra's bearded face appeared in the barn doorway, and he trotted toward them.

"So you stopped by!" he called.

Annie climbed out to shake his hand. "Thank you for everything, Ezra. You have been very kind to us, giving us the benefit of the doubt when you didn't have to."

His grin grew. "I'm glad everything turned out okay."

Mary held out her hand. "Thank you. I will always remember your kindness."

"Oh, I'm being covered with praises this morning," Ezra chuckled. "Did you put these girls up to it, Jesse?"

Everyone laughed. "They are speaking out of their own mouths," Jesse assured him.

The front door burst open and Wauneta hurried down the wooden sidewalk. Annie stepped forward and opened her arms. After a moment's hesitation, she and Wauneta embraced. Mary was right behind her and did the same.

Annie hurried through the story again—of their English Mamm's hopes for her twin girls, and Alisha's happiness for their future Amish lives.

A smile grew on Wauneta's face. "I am so glad to hear it. Sorry for my doubt of your intentions."

"I doubted myself," Annie told her. "But we have done what we set out to do, and now we are heading home."

"As you should be," Wauneta told them. "Mary's Daett must be very worried by now."

No one answered that point as they said their final round of goodbyes. They climbed back into the car and Jesse drove east. The long day's journey back to Lancaster County stretched in front of them.

Twilight was not far away when Jesse pulled his Malibu into Bishop Mast's long driveway. Lily peered ahead. There was no sign of anyone.

"We should go to the house first," Lily decided.

"That won't make things easier," Jesse said, but he still slowed the car.

There was no sound from the back seat. Lily's famous courage had almost failed her if the truth were told.

Jesse parked and Lily hopped out to open the car door for Mary. The poor girl's face was white again, and Lily didn't blame her. Much hung in the balance in these first moments of their arrival, including Mary's future relationship with her Mamm and sister and the plans to have Annie and Alisha attend the wedding—if there was a wedding.

Lily gathered her courage as Bishop Mast stuck his head out of the barn door and charged right for them.

Lily stood her ground. "We will speak with you in the house," she said firmly, before a word could come out of the man's mouth.

"Where have you been with my daughter?" he roared.

Lily took Mary's arm and swept up the sidewalk with her as if she hadn't even heard him.

Bishop Mast glanced from the two occupants of the car to the retreating figures of Lily and his daughter. He huffed and set off after them.

Lily and Mary beat the bishop to the front porch. Rebecca opened the door, and Lily pushed Mary up the steps.

"Oh, Mary!" Rebecca cried and rushed forward to wrap Mary in her arms. "You have come home." Rebecca held Mary at arm's length for a moment. "You still look Amish."

"I am Amish," Mary choked. "I will always be Amish."

"Then why did you leave home?" Bishop Mast thundered behind them. "And what have you been doing?"

Mary turned to face him. "I found my birth Mamm, Daett. Will you hold that against me? Because I know that Ben won't."

"Ben won't what?" Bishop Mast hollered. "Are you threatening me with Ben's displeasure?"

Mary's dress shook below the knees, but she met the bishop's furious gaze. "No, Daett, I wouldn't threaten you. But I will tell Ben everything that happened—and everything that happens now."

"That is threatening me!" Bishop Mast glared at his daughter before turning his wrath on Lily. "And why are you still here, interfering as always?"

She tried not to flinch. "I am sorry that all this has upset you, but we had to find Annie and Mary's Mamm, and we did find her. You should hear the story before you get too upset."

"I don't know how I could be less upset!" The bishop's beard jerked with his words. "After all Mary has put me through—the humiliation, the shame of my daughter disobeying me."

No one made you tell the whole world, Lily almost said, but she bit back the words. "I wish it could have been otherwise, bishop," she said instead, keeping her voice level. "But unless I miss my guess, our community back home will be most happy with how our search turned out, and with what Mary's Mamm had to say. The woman wants nothing more than for her daughters to marry Amish and have the life she never did. Now would you speak against that?"

Bishop Mast turned his baleful eyes on his daughter. "And this is all true?"

"It is true, Daett," Mary replied. "Can you trust me? I love you and Mamm and Ben. I knew you wouldn't let me join Annie and Lily if I asked, but I needed to go with them. I am of age, Daett. I made my choice, and I am the better person for it."

"Listen to your daughter," Rebecca begged, speaking for the first time.

"Let's go inside." Bishop Mast glared around the farm. "The whole world can see us out here."

Lily followed the trio inside. She hadn't been invited, but no one objected either. The rough spots hadn't been traversed yet. She could not leave her sister's twin to face the consequences alone. She was needed to calm Bishop Mast's temper if nothing else. Lily took a deep breath and sat on a chair near the fireplace, while the others settled on the couch. But even as they sat, she knew they would work through this. The bishop's heart would soften, and he would see that it was right for his daughter to maintain a relationship with her birth Mamm and sister. Bishop Mast could not and would not destroy the connection that had been remade between the three women's hearts.

She sighed and allowed herself a small smile. All would be put to rights.

Jesse watched the retreating backs disappear into the house. "Lily is still alive," he chuckled.

"She is so brave," Annie mused. "She has done so much for us on this trip, and now this last effort on Mary's behalf."

Jesse gave Annie a gentle smile. "Lily is your sister, but don't run yourself down. I like you a lot."

Annie ducked her head. "So you came to a decision last night."

"I figured Lily would tell you."

"Where does that leave us?" Annie snuck a glance at him.

His face was grim. "I'm not proud of my past, Annie, nor of how I handled everything on this trip, but I needed to settle the matter in my heart with Lily."

"And you did?"

He nodded.

"So you are going back to the English world?"

He laughed. "No. I will always be Amish."

"Does your decision include me?"

"Do you want it to?"

"My heart does. I'm staying in the community. Is that enough?"

"Nothing will happen suddenly, and we both have a long walk toward healing. But yah, I am ready for the journey." The words sounded choked. "Sorry, but that was hard for me to say. I vowed once I would never love again."

"Then you do? Love me? I thought you were just saying that in Ezra's barn."

"I love you far too much, Annie," he whispered. "Far too much already."

Her fingers intertwined with his. "You surely know that I'll never quite be an Amish girl. I mean, I'll try, but in my heart I'll still be an English girl adopted by the Amish. That is a difference I may never be able to overcome."

Jesse stilled her lips with a touch of his finger. "I love you, Annie, just the way you are. I don't understand how it will work—you and me. Not exactly. But the road is open. I will walk with you, if you will walk with me?"

"Are you proposing?" Annie forced a laugh.

He joined in. "Stating my intentions, that's all. If that's your heart too, we can begin our plans together."

"My search is over—I've found my Mamm, my sister, and my love. My heart is so full it might burst." She reached for him. "Kiss me, Jesse."

"We shouldn't," he warned. "The bishop might look out the window. We don't want to disrupt the fragile negotiations."

"I won't take no for an answer," she warned.

His eyes twinkled. "Just to be sure about this first—will you marry me, Annie Miller? Or plan to, at least?"

She smiled up at him and nestled against his shoulder. "I will, Jesse Yoder. I will stay with our Amish life, and I will make my home with you, whenever you are ready."

Jesse pulled Annie close and held her tight in the twilight silence of Bishop Mast's farm. As he kissed her tenderly, Annie knew her search—like their journey—was finally at an end.